BEFORE THE LAST LAP
A Sharyn Howard Mystery

Tracey J. Lyons

This time the mystery for Sheriff Sharyn Howard and her Diamond Springs deputies hits a little bit closer to home. After a speeding boat flies up over the pier and onto the street, the sheriff's department investigates. They become personally involved when the pocketbook of Sharyn's assistant, Trudy Robinson, is found on the boat—along with a lot of blood. Trudy has been missing for days, and things don't look promising.

While combing the crime scene at the boat a dead body washes up beside the pier. Upon discovering that the dead man was the head mechanic for a local racecar driver, Sharyn's investigation turns to the speedway. Could legendary driver Duke Beatty be the one behind it all? Sharyn has her suspicions.

Trudy is found unharmed at the speedway at the same time that Duke is shot and killed, and it appears that she may be the murderer. Trudy's husband, Ed, one of Sharyn's deputies who also happened to be on the scene at the time, tries to protect his wife by claiming that he is guilty of shooting Duke.

Now Sharyn must prove that Ed is innocent while also trying to find the real culprit.

Other books by Joyce and Jim Lavene:

The *Sharyn Howard Mystery* Series:

Last Dance
One Last Good-bye
The Last to Remember
Until Our Last Embrace
For the Last Time
Dreams Don't Last
Last Fires Burning
Glory's Last Victim
Last Rites
Last One Down

Also writing as Joye Ames:

A Time for Love
If Not for You
Only You
Save Your Heart for Me
The Dowager Duchess
Madison's Miracles

BEFORE THE LAST LAP

•

Joyce and Jim Lavene

AVALON BOOKS
NEW YORK

PRINTED IN THE UNITED STATES OF AMERICA
ON ACID-FREE PAPER
BY HADDON CRAFTSMEN, BLOOMSBURG, PENNSYLVANIA

For NASCAR fans and small town heroes everywhere!

Prologue

The two fishermen were enjoying the late September night in Diamond Springs. The golden harvest moon rose across Diamond Mountain Lake, gilding the smooth surface. The bass were biting and their buckets were full. Still they lingered, talking about nothing, listening to the quiet town around them.

"What's that?" The sound from the lake was muffled but growing steadily louder.

"Don't know," came the answer, "tourist season is over. Besides, nobody races a boat at night."

"That's a boat for sure," the other man persisted, getting slowly to his feet. He squinted across the two-mile expanse of lake but didn't see any lights. "Where's she coming in at?"

"I'm telling you, that's not a boat." The second man pushed to his feet, mindful of the bucket beside him where the fish still splashed from time to time. "Probably a plane. One of those prop jobs."

"Sounds like it's heading right for us. You don't think it's like Captain Billy Bost, do you? About to drop into the lake?"

"Don't be stupid. Get your stuff and let's go home."

When the chrome on the fast moving boat was finally close enough to glint in the lights that hung over the pier, it was too late to do anything but jump out of the way. The boat

1

hit the pier and used it as a ramp. It leaped twenty feet in the air and came down in the middle of the street behind the pier. A car immediately crashed into it. Then everything was silent again.

"Holy Hannah!" one of the fishermen exclaimed as he watched from the cool lake water. "What was that?"

Chapter One

"Well, aren't you a sight?"

Sheriff Sharyn Howard ignored the remark as she ducked under the yellow police tape. She was in a yellow and brown Burger King uniform, complete with a brown ball cap she forgot to remove. Her curly, copper-red hair poked out around the edges of the cap and she had a grease smudge on her nose. "I hope this is important, Chief. I was almost through my shift. Now I'll have to work through another one."

Diamond Springs Police Chief Roy Tarnower laughed. His heavy jowls shook on his bulldog face. "That's right. Your response to that meatball in the *Gazette*, who said your job wasn't as tough as his was for even one shift. That was inspired, Sheriff. I think I would've managed to talk my way out of it."

"It wasn't so bad. What happened here?" She looked at the two wrecks in the street. "Somebody lose a boat?"

"I'm calling it boat versus car. Can't do a blamed thing until the fish and wildlife people get here. The boat jumped out of the lake and hit the street. That makes it their jurisdiction. Then the car hit the boat. That makes it *mine*."

Sharyn had lived in Diamond Springs all of her life but she had never heard of a boat jumping out of the lake. That was a new one. Medical personnel were treating the two

3

people in the late model Honda. It was impossible to see into the boat from her angle in the street since it was resting on top of the car. "Was anyone in the boat?"

"Not so far as we can tell." The chief spat on the ground. "I've got a call in to the ME's office. They take a right long while to respond. Surprised you haven't singed their ears on that by now."

"When classes are in session at the college, Nick is slower." After being sheriff of Diamond Springs and Montgomery County, North Carolina for almost five years with the same medical examiner, she knew the process. Roy had been police chief of the small town in the Uwharrie Mountains for less than a year. It would probably take him a while to understand how it worked. Luckily, the town was quiet most of the time. He wouldn't need the medical examiner very often.

Nick Thomopolis drove up as she was thinking about him. He climbed out of his SUV with his black bag in hand. Sharyn could tell he'd been grading papers. When he was frustrated, he had a way of running his fingers through his thick salt and pepper hair that left it spiked up on his head. That usually only happened during a murder investigation or when he was grading some bad test papers.

"I didn't expect to see you here." He kissed her forehead and slid his free arm around her waist. "Yummy. You smell like burgers. I hope you brought some home."

She smiled at him. "Sorry. I didn't get to close up so they didn't give me any leftovers. Maybe next time."

"Liked it so well you're staying?"

"No," she answered quietly. "Didn't finish the shift. Tomorrow the *Gazette* will announce I couldn't take it and left early. The only way is to go back for a whole shift."

"You're too sensitive to criticism. Who cares what some college kid thinks about your job? Let's take him up on Sweet Potato Mountain and let him try to get down on foot with someone trying to kill him like you over the summer. I think *that* would be a better comparison."

Sharyn knew he was probably right, but those memories

were too fresh to think about for long. Besides, Roy was listening in with an overeager expression on his face. He was the biggest gossip in town. "Anyway, I'm here. But I'm not sure *why* I'm here." She glanced at the chief for an explanation.

Roy put his meaty fists on his hips and cocked his head. "This is a courtesy call, Sheriff Howard. As you know, I'm not obligated to inform you when something happens in the city proper. But in this case, I thought you might be interested."

"Thanks, Chief. It's *really* interesting but—"

"I think this pertains to one of your current cases, Sheriff. Ms. Trudy Robinson. Her pocketbook is in the back of the boat, along with a considerable amount of blood. But no sign of Ms. Robinson."

"Hey, Chief!" Officer David Matthews called out to his boss. "There's a man floating in the lake. Should we fish him out?"

The squat police chief looked at Nick, who answered, "I guess so. I'm not going in after him."

"Grab a hook and do that, David. Lay him out on the pier," Tarnower told his officer.

Nick squeezed Sharyn's waist a little. "Maybe this is the lead you've been looking for with Trudy. Are you going to call Ed?"

She shook her head. "Not yet. I want to get some idea of what's going on before I tell him. He's been edgy and strange the last few days."

"If my wife was missing, I'd be edgy and strange too."

"I expected him to be," she agreed. "I just don't want to get him all worked up for nothing."

"Okay. Let me take a look at the body then we'll see what we can find out about the boat. The van should be here soon. I'll be as fast as I can."

"Would you like some help until Megan and Keith get here?" she asked. "I'm not in charge on this like usual. I could give you a hand."

He studied her face. "Are you sure? It's kind of demeaning for a sheriff to become a medical examiner's assistant. Even if she *is* wearing a burger-flipping uniform."

"It would make it faster, wouldn't it? If this involves Trudy, I want to know right away."

"Yeah." He took a deep breath. "Let's go."

David and one of the other officers dragged the man out of the water as Sharyn and Nick reached the end of the pier. Nick wordlessly handed her a pair of latex gloves and a notebook. He knelt beside the body on the wet pier and took a few pictures. The smell of fish and lake water competed with the heavy aroma of gasoline from the crash. It was amazing that the boat or the car didn't catch fire.

"He's male. Probably in his early thirties. Dark brown hair. About one hundred and fifty pounds."

Sharyn crouched beside Nick and wrote what he said in the notebook. The man on the pier looked familiar but she couldn't place him. The thought nagged at her that she'd questioned him about something a few years back. But *that* group included too many people for her to recall.

It was difficult to concentrate on the dead man when the answer to Trudy's disappearance might be in the speedboat. Trudy Robinson was her assistant at the sheriff's department. She'd been missing for three days. Her husband, Deputy Ed Robinson, was frantically searching for her. He'd gone to sleep with her on Sunday night. The next morning, she was gone.

At first, they all thought the recently married couple had an argument. Trudy left to clear her mind. Then they found her car on the Interstate. The hours passed and the entire department grew more worried. Trudy was hired by Sharyn's father, Sheriff T. Raymond Howard. She was the backbone of the department. She always knew what was going on. She kept everything and everyone in order.

She was married to her high school sweetheart, Ben, for thirty years and had four children with him. But her life had gone through some radical changes in recent years. Ben was killed in a race car accident.

Everyone suspected foul play, but an investigation didn't support that theory. Then Trudy eloped with Ed last spring, despite knowing his reputation as a veteran flirt. She even suggested she'd like to become a deputy, making it clear she longed for something more than her desk job. No one took her seriously. Maybe that was part of the problem.

"Did you get that?" Nick nudged Sharyn with his elbow.

Her brain hurried back to the pier. "Sorry. What did you say?"

"I ordered a Big Beefy and a large Coke." He sighed. "I thought Megan was bad. When did you zone out?"

"After you said what he weighed."

"Okay. After that, I said he's about six feet tall and has a single bullet wound in his back. The blood in the boat might belong to him. He's only been dead a few hours. I don't think he drowned. Maybe he was piloting the boat. Someone shot him. He fell out and the boat flew up here."

"Not so fast," she complained. "I'm not a computer."

"Just trying to keep you awake."

"Sharyn! Nick!" Bruce Bellows, Montgomery County's head wildlife official, joined them. "I'm glad you're here. I don't have a whole lot of people killed in my jurisdiction. Once or twice a year a hunter will accidentally shoot himself or somebody else. That's about it. I don't know what to say about this."

"Hi, Bruce." Sharyn removed one glove as she got to her feet. She shook his hand. "Where's Sam?"

"He's staying out at your aunt's house. She's harvesting herbs or some such. I didn't want to call him unless I had to." He smiled at her, his earnest face worried. "Should I call him?"

"There's not really any reason to," she said. "Chief Tarnower needs you to give him your okay to move the body and the boat. He'll take it from there."

He was obviously relieved. "I'm glad about that. I'm good with anything that has four feet. I'm even okay with snakes. But I'm not much good with people. You know that. Sam's better but that's not saying a lot. Sometimes I think the only reason he gets along is half the time he's mumbling in Cherokee and they can't understand him."

She laughed. Sam Two-Rivers was a good friend. He'd worked with the sheriff's department as a tracker. Recently, he'd taken up with her Aunt Selma. They were a perfect match. "I think you're right. The chief is over there by the Honda. Have him sign you off on this and you should be able to go home."

"Thanks. Any news about Trudy yet? I saw the television ad offering the reward for information. I know Ed must be crazy by now."

She didn't want to say anything since reporters had begun to gather around the accident site. "We're looking for her. All we can do right now is pray she's still alive."

"No ransom demand?"

"Not yet. I'll tell Ed you asked about them."

"Thanks, Sharyn. Let me know if there's anything I can do. Good luck out here."

Nick got to his feet. "The kids are here. There's not a lot of crime scene on the pier. Let me have the body moved to the morgue. We'll take a look at the boat."

"Any ID on the body?" She put her glove back on.

"No. Nothing on him at all. You know, you're not supposed to do that," he mentioned. "Once the gloves go on, they're supposed to stay on until you're done. I'm surprised you don't know that, being sheriff and all. You could've contaminated the crime scene."

"I only touched Bruce," she argued. "Unless he's part of the crime scene, I think we're okay."

"I'll let you get away with it this time. But don't let it happen again."

She rolled her eyes as she followed him to the boat. "I'm glad I don't work for you."

"Why? I'm easy to work for. Follow the rules. Don't throw your stuff on the floor. It's not that hard."

"That's not what Megan tells me. Anyway, I know better. I've worked *with* you. You're a pain in the neck. If I didn't love you, I wouldn't go out with you either."

"I hope not. Well, you'd at least have to *like* me anyway. Unless you were dating me for my flashy SUV and my unique gun collection. Not to mention my considerable good looks and charm."

"If I vomit now, you can't blame it on the dead body." She laughed. "Did anyone ever date you because of your guns or car?"

"What about my other attributes? The guns and the car are secondary."

"Keep telling yourself that, Nick. We'll both pretend it's true."

Their banter put off the hard job ahead of them. They stood at the side of the narrow yellow boat. It was specially designed and modified to race on the water. Police officers were using jacks to stabilize it so the crime scene crew could get inside.

"Aren't these illegal on the lake?" Nick asked Sharyn as they waited for the officers to finish.

"County commission passed an ordinance two years ago against them. These cigarette boats have five-hundred horse-power engines or better. A lot of people think they go too fast on a lake that has so much traffic."

"That's too fast for me. Of course, I don't think anything should travel on water." He peered over the side of the craft. "Looks like the glove box is open. Maybe we'll find some ID there."

Chief Tarnower came to stand beside them, his arms fold-ed across his blue-uniformed chest. "Any idea who the floater was? Was he in the boat?"

"I can't tell what went on in the boat until I get inside it," Nick explained. "I appreciate your belief in my near super-human powers of deduction, Chief. But even I have to look around. I didn't recognize the man on the pier. I'll check the boat for ID. If that doesn't work, we'll send out his picture and see what comes up."

The officers signaled that the boat was stable. The fire department crew put a ladder up against the hull. Sharyn climbed up first, careful not to step in the blood that covered half of the bottom of the boat. The white cushion seats were splattered with it. So was Trudy's brown pocketbook.

She waited until Nick could follow her, dreading what

they might find in the hold. She didn't want to investigate the murder of another person she loved. Her career as sheriff began that way. Her father was murdered in a convenience store robbery. She'd put aside her emotions and concentrated on finding his killers. They were caught and convicted, although later events caused her to question if she actually put the *right* men in prison.

There was so much blood in the boat. It reminded her of seeing her father on the concrete floor, surrounded by a sea of his blood.

Memories of Trudy flooded into her mind. She always had a kind smile and a cold Pepsi for Sharyn when she was a child. After her father died, Sharyn relied on Trudy and Ernie in those first difficult years as sheriff. She didn't want to think what she was going to do without her. Just the idea that the blood could be Trudy's made her want to fall down and cry.

Nick climbed up in the boat and put his arm around her. "Are you okay?"

She didn't see him come over the side. She didn't realize how long she'd been standing there, staring at the blood. She looked at him, not seeing his handsome Greek features or his dark, worried eyes. "I'm fine."

"Just because Trudy's purse is here doesn't mean this is her blood," he reminded her. "This guy could've stolen her purse. That might be the only connection."

"Thanks. Sorry to hold you up." She glanced at his hands. "You took your gloves off before you were done. I don't know if I can let that go without reporting you to the medical examiners' conference or something."

"You're a pain in the neck *and* you have a smart mouth. You don't have many guns. You don't even have an SUV. I don't know what I see in you."

"It's the uniform," she assured him. "It turns all the men on."

He laughed. "Would that be the burger uniform or the sheriff's uniform?"

"Are we going to work here or are we going to talk all night?"

"That was just comic relief." He put fresh gloves on. "Let's get this over with."

Sharyn took pictures while Nick collected blood samples from various parts of the boat. She hated to be impatient. She knew forensic collection was a lengthy, time consuming process. It was important to eventually solving the crime. It required patience and a keen eye. All of those attributes Nick seemed to have in abundance. Ones she mostly lacked.

All she wanted to do was examine the pocketbook and hope it could lead her to Trudy. Nick was taking the evidence according to its importance. The pocketbook wouldn't dry up or be washed away if it rained. It would be bagged and tagged for study in the lab. Everything he did was rational, purposeful.

She kept glancing at the far end of the boat, dropping the plastic evidence bags twice as she was labeling them. Nick finally opened the hold. There was nothing there but some rope and a flashlight. She took a deep breath. That was a relief. Still the purse waited, weighing heavily on her thoughts.

"Careful!" He frowned at her when she moved a bag before he could put hair samples into it. "This evidence is important too."

"I *know* that." Sharyn's temper and impatience laced her words. "I'm not doing it on purpose."

"Quit looking at Trudy's purse. We're not going to get there any faster because you're staring at it. It won't grow legs and run away."

"I don't know how you do this. I never realized how patient you have to be. I never really think of you as being a patient, methodical man but I guess you are."

He paused, halfway to the front of the boat, holding a fiber sample he'd lifted from one of the seats. "If I *wasn't* patient, I would've given up on you years ago. You've been my greatest challenge."

"Not *years*. You didn't even like me when I started as sheriff. You were nasty and sarcastic with me. It was like working with a bear. You were going to quit. I still have a copy of your resignation."

"Because I couldn't see you every day and not tell you how I felt. I'm patient. Not dead."

"That's *so* sweet." She smiled at him and kissed his cheek. "Now can we move on to Trudy's pocketbook?"

Nick groaned, knowing he'd never win. "I'll give you one thing. You may not have enough patience to stuff an acorn, but you're certainly focused. It must be the red hair."

"Knowing that," she agreed, "could we move this along a little? I know you have certain ways of doing things. I know the protocol. But this involves *Trudy*. I have even less patience tonight."

The boat moved under them. Megan's head popped up on the side. "Permission to come aboard, sir?" She saw Sharyn and stopped popping her gum. "Hey! What's *she* doing here? This is *my* job."

"And just in time." Nick took the samples from Sharyn. "I'm sure there's someplace else you should be." He handed the samples to Megan. "You can store these then get started on dusting the steering area or whatever nautical term there is for it. Is Keith here too?"

"Yeah," Megan answered, still glaring at Sharyn. "He's bringing up some gear. Sorry we're late. The van wouldn't start again. We came in Keith's car."

"That van is a piece of junk," he remarked. "We need to get some money from the commission for a new one."

Sharyn teased him. "You're so fickle. First you want my help. Then she comes along and you want her."

"No offense," he began, "but at least she knows what she's doing. And she hardly ever drops the evidence or doesn't pay attention. She even *likes* working on dead bodies."

"Sounds like the perfect woman for you. Maybe she'd appreciate your gun collection too."

He seemed to consider the idea. "No. It wouldn't work. She's not good at putting herself in harm's way. She doesn't have gorgeous red hair or a killer smile that knocks me down when I see her. You can't get rid of me that easy."

Megan's smile was brilliant as she stood beside Nick. "Nice uniform, Sheriff. But I think you should complain to the commission. These new uniforms make you look like you work at a burger joint or something." She laughed, a hyena-like sound that ended in a snort.

Sharyn knew it was time for her to leave. All she could do *legally* was wait for Nick to evaluate what he found. The murder investigation belonged to Chief Tarnower. She had no reason to be there. But Trudy's pocketbook, and all the secrets it might hold, taunted her. She didn't want to wait for second-hand information.

The boat pitched again and Keith's head popped up on the side. "Hey, Sheriff."

"Hey, Keith." Seeing him gave Sharyn a desperate idea. She knew it might make Nick angry beside it being against procedure. She didn't care. Making her choice, she took the single step she needed to reach Trudy's pocketbook.

"Hey!" Megan's voice screeched. "Sharyn's stealing evidence!"

Nick looked where she pointed. "What are you doing? You know better."

"What?" Sharyn tried to look innocent. "The boat started rocking and I was thrown this way. I didn't mean to pick up the pocketbook. But since I have it . . ."

He snatched the little leather satchel from her. "You know I can't let you take this. What are you trying to do, ruin the chain of evidence?"

"I'm trying to find Trudy! Either look at the pocketbook *now* or I'm taking it with me. I want some answers *tonight*."

An angry frown hovered around his mouth. "Yes, ma'am. You're the sheriff. Even if this isn't *your* case."

Sharyn watched as he started slowly taking everything out of the pocketbook. She knew he was angry. For a few seconds, she wasn't sure if he would agree to examine it. He would've rejected a similar demand from Roy. She didn't like presuming on their relationship but this was important to her.

"I've got some tissues, a nail file. Are you getting this?"

She scrambled to find some paper and a pen after giving hers to Megan. But before she could locate anything, the young ME's assistant elbowed her way between them. "I'll get this. Thanks anyway, Sheriff."

Nick ignored them and continued cataloguing the contents of the pocketbook. "Her wallet's in here. It has her driver's license, social security card, two credit cards and a hundred dollars in cash."

Megan scrawled the words on the paper. Sharyn tapped her foot impatiently. Keith finally managed to climb inside the boat.

Nick told him to start dusting for prints as he continued cataloging. "There's some makeup. A book of matches. A pen. And a half package of peanut butter crackers. That's about it."

"That's all there is in the wallet?" Sharyn asked. "What about the outside compartment?"

He opened the outside zippered section and pulled out a single piece of paper. "This is it. Nothing else. We'll dust it for prints. Check it for GSR."

"What does it say?" She could see the writing on the paper but couldn't read it.

"Bread, eggs, milk." He shrugged. "Looks like a shopping list."

"Thanks for looking. Could you send me a copy of whatever you find here when you send to the Chief? I know the homicide is out of my jurisdiction—"

"Will do."

"Nick," she started to explain, but he had already moved off to the front of the boat to join Keith.

"Now you've done it, sweetie," Megan hissed as she sauntered by. "He's *mad*. It takes a lot to make him mad. You'll probably be hearing about it for the next six months."

Sharyn smiled at her as she started climbing over the side of the boat. "You know, the thing about Nick? He likes to take it out on the people he works with. Sorry, *sweetie*."

Megan's thin face drooped as she acknowledged the truth. She played with her purple braids, adjusted her heavy glasses and turned away.

Sheriff's deputies Ed Robinson and Ernie Watkins were waiting in the street. News of finding Trudy's pocketbook in the boat reached them quickly. They were straining against the police officers trying to control the curious crowd when they saw Sharyn. She urged them away from the accident scene.

"I can't believe this," Ed growled, glancing back. "My wife's pocketbook is in the boat, covered in blood, and I can't get up there. I *knew* separating the town and county law enforcement was stupid. I didn't know *how* stupid it was until now. This should've been *our* case!"

"Best thing we can do is get away from here," Ernie said. "They'll let us know when they have something."

Sharyn kept them walking up the steep hill that led away from the lake. "I saw what was in Trudy's pocketbook. But I didn't want to share it with anyone else until we have a chance to check it out."

Ed stopped walking. His curly blond hair looked white in the streetlight's glow. His eyes were haunted, shadows accentuating the dark circles under them. "If you know something, Sharyn, spit it out. I don't care who else knows."

"That's because you're not thinking right," she told him. "Let's go up to my place. We'll talk about it there and decide what to do."

Her apartment was only a block away. Ed agreed after a little extra urging from Ernie. They sat around her small kitchen table as she made coffee for them. While she worked, she explained everything she knew about what happened to the boat.

"So we're not any closer to finding her?" Ed demanded, the blue of his jogging suit matching his eyes.

"Everyone is doing the best they can." Ernie's mustache twitched. "Use your head instead of your gut or you're no good to us."

Ed shot to his feet. "Don't say that to me! Nobody snatched Annie out of your bed. My wife is gone. She might be dead. I can't rationalize this."

"I'm sorry," Ernie was quick to apologize. "I love Trudy too. We all do. We'll figure out what happened to her."

Sharyn poured coffee into three mugs shaped like chickens. She put out chicken-shaped containers of milk and sugar. Both men stared at their mugs without touching them. "What's wrong?"

"I would've never picked you for a chicken collector." Ernie turned his mug around to look at it.

"Yeah," Ed agreed with a reluctant smile. "It's kind of embarrassing. The sheriff of Montgomery County serves coffee in chickens."

"I could just pour it in your hand if that would help," she offered, sitting down with them. "Okay. Ed, we've talked about this since Trudy went missing. Let's talk about it again. Did you notice her acting strange? Did she go off by herself a lot lately?"

"We've only been married a few months," he explained. "You know that. Newlyweds don't tend to go off by themselves much."

"What about her other actions?" Ernie suggested. "Any unusual phone calls? Anything you noticed out of the ordinary?"

Ed sipped his coffee and tried to recall . . . again. "You know, there *was* an article in the *Gazette* that night. She ran to the kitchen and cut it out. I didn't pay much attention at the time. I don't think it means anything."

"Just drop the dramatic buildup and tell us," Sharyn urged. "What happened?"

"There was another serious injury at the speedway. She cuts articles about that stuff. I think it's because of Ben being killed out there. She was interested in anything to do with the racetrack. She went out there every Saturday night until we were married."

"Why didn't you tell us before?" Ernie lifted the chicken creamer and added more milk to his coffee.

"What good does it do?" Ed's voice was ragged. "What difference did it make if she cut out an article about the track? I'm already talking about her like she's dead."

"Maybe no difference," Sharyn stopped him. "But maybe it can point us in the right direction."

"She didn't disappear on Saturday night," Ed reminded her. "It's not like she got up in the middle of the night and went to the track. Someone took her."

Ernie and Sharyn exchanged glances. She sipped her coffee while Ernie re-stated the facts. "There was no sign of forced entry into your house. There was no sign of a struggle. Trudy's car keys, purse and cell phone were missing. Her nightgown was folded neatly on her side of the bed. She got up and went somewhere, Ed. The sooner you accept that the sooner we can help her."

Ed blinked back tears. "She didn't leave me. She *wouldn't* leave me alone like that. I don't believe it. Someone made her do this."

"Someone may have coerced her." Sharyn tried to calm him. "I think we should go back to your house and look at everything again. Let's find out how many articles Trudy kept about the speedway. Maybe if we look at that, we can figure out where she went. Maybe she was looking for something or someone related to the speedway?"

"It's worth a shot," Ed replied. "But I know she told me everything. It's not like she was sneaking around. I think you're in the wrong lane, Sheriff. But anything beats sitting around thinking about it."

Ernie clapped him on the shoulder. "We don't know *any* of that blood on the boat belongs to Trudy, old son. In my mind, she's still alive and waiting for us to find her."

"Then let's get going." Sharyn got to her feet. "We've only got a few hours before we have to go to work. Maybe we can find what we need and bring Trudy home today."

Chapter Two

"I don't know what we're looking for." Ed dropped down on the green sofa in his living room. "Trudy doesn't keep secrets. Both of you know her. She isn't like that."

Sharyn and Ernie sank into chairs near him. They scoured the house for another hour. The entire sheriff's department was there after Trudy disappeared. Nick and his team went over the house. There was nothing more tonight than there was two days ago.

"Let's go through that night one more time." Sharyn rubbed her tired eyes with her hands. "You came home from work at about seven-thirty."

Ed nodded. "That's right. We went out to dinner at Fuigi's after work. We had pasta primavera and those little meat-balls. I had salad and she had soup. We didn't have any wine. She drank water like she always does. I drank—"

"Come on, Ed." Ernie sat forward in his chair. He pushed his glasses back against his face. "I know we've been over this a hundred times but let's try to focus one more time."

"Okay! We came home. Checked the mail. Trudy looked through the newspaper like she always does. I watched some sports on TV. She was in the kitchen for a while. I don't know what she was doing in there. Making lunches or something. She came in here with me after a while. We watched

18

one of those shows with the couples on it. She likes those. Then we went to bed."

"And you noticed she was gone when you woke up to go to the bathroom a little after midnight," Sharyn encouraged. "What did you do?"

"I looked through the house for her. When I couldn't find her in here, I looked in the garage. Her car was gone. I called her sister and her mother. I called the kids. No one had seen her or heard from her."

Sharyn picked up the newspaper that rested on top of Trudy's crochet bag. "Is this what she cut out that night?" She glanced through the sports section. A large column-sized space was cut out. The newspaper was dated the day Trudy disappeared.

Ed looked at the paper. "Yeah. She took it in the kitchen with her."

"That's one place we *didn't* look for newspaper clippings." Ernie got to his feet with all the wiry spring of a slinky. "I'll check around in there."

"I'll see if I can talk to someone at the *Gazette* night desk," Sharyn volunteered. "Maybe they can tell me what was in this space."

"Maybe she kept those articles in her cookbooks." Ed joined Ernie. "She's always cutting out something and putting it in her cookbooks. I thought it was recipes. You know how she likes to try new food."

There was no one at the night news desk at the *Diamond Springs Gazette,* the only newspaper in the area. Sharyn left a message on voice mail. The chances were good there was only one person manning the desk at night. He or she was probably out covering the boat in the middle of the street. That would probably be the story of the month. Not many boats flew out of the lake or left dead men behind in the water.

"We found it," Ernie called out from the kitchen. "She kept them in the pantry."

Sharyn joined them in the small pantry. The naked light bulb above their heads caused dancing shadows on the walls and floor as it swung back and forth on a long cord from the ceiling. Most of the walls were covered in canned goods. There were large bags of rice, cans of pinto beans, and plenty of macaroni and cheese. But the back wall was plastered with newspaper articles. The earliest one was news of Ben's death at the speedway.

"Sheriff Sharyn Howard is investigating, but so far no criminal intent has been found," she read aloud from the article about Trudy's husband's death. It was strange to look back on that case. It seemed like so long ago.

"Remember? There was a question about Jack Winter messing around in that," Ernie said. "Ben told animal control about those horses Jack was underfeeding. We looked into it. There wasn't any evidence Jack had anything to do with Ben's death."

Ed touched the picture, yellowed and faded. It was a photo of Trudy, standing beside Ben's grave. "Not that we didn't look real hard. We all wanted Jack for that one. But unless we made something up, he was clean."

"So what was she thinking?" Ernie squinted at the articles taped to the wall. "Was she just interested in accidents at the speedway because Ben died there?"

"I don't know," Ed admitted. "We never talked about it. I can't believe we've been married all this time and I didn't know. I guess I've never been in here with the light on."

Ernie frowned at him. "Never?"

"Well, you don't need the light on to grab a jar of peanut butter." Ed showed him. "It's near the door."

"If it makes you feel any better," Sharyn continued while looking over the articles, "she started collecting these before you were married, which by the way, hasn't been that long."

"But why?" Ed looked at the articles again. "What was she trying to do?"

"You don't suppose she was trying to continue the investigation on her own, do you?" Ernie asked them. "Could she still be looking for more information to prove Ben was murdered?"

"That's possible," Sharyn said. "All of the articles pertain to Duke Beatty. Maybe she thought he was involved."

"Duke?" Ernie laughed. "Old Duke didn't have any reason to kill Ben. They were both drivers, but Ben wasn't in Duke's league at all. He was a weekend racer. Trudy was climbing up the wrong tree if she thought that."

She glanced at her watch as the alarm went off. "I have to get home, take a shower and change. This is all we can do right now. Maybe Nick will have something else for us as the day goes on. We've got Trudy's pocketbook. Maybe it means we're one step closer to finding her."

Ed turned off the light in the pantry. "Thanks for helping me with this. I guess I'll see you at the office."

"Like you could've kept us from helping." Ernie shook Ed's hand. "You and Trudy are kin. We'll find her."

"You don't have to come in today." Sharyn hugged Ed but didn't like the haggard look to his face. "Nobody would blame you. You know we'll check out every lead we can. We'll get the right tip and she'll be there. You'll see."

"I know." He smiled at her and ruffled her hair. "But I want to be there. All I'd do out here is sit around and think about it. That's all I've been doing since she disappeared. But I appreciate the offer. You make me feel so old when you sound so mature and understanding."

She laughed and squeezed his hand. "All right. I'll see you later."

She and Ernie headed back toward Diamond Springs. Trudy and Ed lived further out in the county, between Diamond Springs and Frog Meadow. Ed sold his small house to move in with Trudy after they were married. Trudy and Ben raised their children in the big, white farmhouse. Her kids were grown now, adults with their own families. Now it was just Trudy and Ed.

"I forgot to call Annie and tell her I was going over to Ed's house." Ernie took out his cell phone and punched in her number.

"How long are the two of you going to wait to get married?"

There was a long silence between them as they drove down the deserted county road. The leaves on the trees were starting to turn red and yellow on the edge of the road. It was a wet fall this year, thank goodness. No wild fires in the mountains.

Ernie left a message on Annie's voicemail and closed his phone. "Guess she's not up yet."

Sharyn applied her brake as a raccoon scurried across the road. "That's not surprising since it's barely five. I doubt if she goes in to school that early. Are you pretending you didn't hear my question?"

"No, not exactly. I'm surprised at you asking since *every-one* wants to know the same thing about you and Nick. You're the one person I expected to be safe with."

"I don't think so. Nick and I weren't almost married and I don't live in the guesthouse on his property. I think that's different."

He shrugged his thin shoulders. The single sprig of dark hair on top of his head was standing straight up. Usually his hat kept it down. "Busybody."

"Procrastinator."

"There's no need to swear at me, Sheriff." He grinned at her. "Just because your daddy isn't here doesn't mean I can't give you a whipping."

Sharyn had known Ernie all of her life. Between the lines of good humor was a serious wish not to answer her question. He and Annie had been back together about six months after personal doubts had caused him to cancel their wedding plans. He moved into the tiny guesthouse when they got back together. He sold his house before the wedding and had been living from motel to Sharyn's apartment for a while.

"You really think Nick might have something on that pocketbook today?" Ernie asked as she dropped him off at the end of Annie's driveway. Puffs of fog surrounded him, blurring the bend in the drive. The strange earthy smell of dying vegetation was pungent in the morning air.

"I hope so. We both know disappearances that go on too long don't end well. We have to find Trudy soon."

"I'll see you at the office then." He smiled, the ends of his mustache lifting. "And just for good measure, Annie and I are thinking about getting married next summer. Not that you *deserve* to know after butting in on my personal life."

"Thanks." She didn't have to ask why they were waiting so long. She knew Ernie was worried this time after the last disaster.

"What about you and Nick?" His eyes gleamed behind his glasses. "When is the happy day for you?"

"We really don't have anything planned," she admitted. "I guess we like things the way they are. For now, anyway. Who knows by next summer?"

"Thanks for nothing." He shook his finger at her. "I better not read about it in the *Gazette* before I hear it from you."

"You won't," she promised. "See you later."

Sharyn drove through the empty streets of Diamond Springs. Rain from the day before had washed a pattern of colored leaves into the streets. The old lady houses watched over Main Street, gossiping to each other through their gingerbread eaves. Lights were on in the new police station. Caterers were moving food and decorations inside for the official dedication that would take place later that day.

The 'new' Diamond Springs police station used to be the home of the sheriff's department. The county commission decided to use the building next to the modern pink granite courthouse for the police department when they created the new law enforcement unit that patrolled the city. They began work on a new building for the sheriff's department. It was only a few blocks down but wouldn't be completed for another year or so.

In the meantime, the sheriff's department was located in the basement of the courthouse. It was inconvenient, crowded and musty. But at least the commission didn't move the new sheriff's building out of Diamond Springs. That was the only good thing Sharyn could find to say about the arrangement.

The commission picked up the tab for major renovations on the police station. Today was its official grand reopening, complete with helium balloons, hot dogs and plenty of free Pepsi from the local distributor. Chief Roy Tarnower would smile for the cameras and the last remnants of the old sheriff's office would be history.

Sharyn Howard was the third generation of law enforcement in Diamond Springs. She was the first woman ever to be elected as sheriff in the state of North Carolina. She followed her grandfather, Jacob Howard, who was the first sheriff elected in Montgomery County and her father, T. Raymond Howard. She was also the first sheriff kicked out of the town to patrol the county roads and handle crimes outside the city limits.

Sometimes it seemed like a good thing. With the new Interstate came new people and new businesses. The crime rate soared almost as fast as new subdivisions sprang up in the county. At the same time, tourists began to discover the clean city with a lake in its heart, surrounded by the beautiful, mysterious Uwharrie Mountains. The past summer was the biggest crowd ever. Sharyn had her hands full with the county. She knew Roy felt the same about Diamond Springs.

She still felt a little cheated sometimes. This was *her* town. She grew up here, lived here. She loved every street with a fierce passion. It was difficult for her to step back and let Roy take over the law enforcement of Diamond Springs. It wasn't a logical response to the situation. The logical part of her brain was constantly at war with the part that was still a little girl looking up at her daddy the sheriff with pride, knowing he protected their home.

She parked the Jeep outside her apartment building. All she could see of the accident scene a block down by the lake, was a wrecker towing away the damaged red Honda. She hadn't thought about giving up patrolling the city for weeks. It had to be the accident that morning, playing second fiddle to Roy in an investigation important to her, that made her heart ache with it again. She needed some coffee and a low carb bar. Then she'd feel better.

Sharyn yawned and let herself into her apartment. She'd only been living on her own for a short while. Her mother, Faye Howard, still wasn't adjusted to it. She called every day and constantly brought food over for her. Since she knew a steady diet of her mother's cooking had led to her being thirty pounds overweight, Sharyn usually got rid of the food. Ernie was always glad to take it. He could eat the heavy cream sauces and fried everything and never gain a pound.

She supposed it was as hard for her mother to make the switch from a house full of people to living by herself as it was for her to give up being sheriff of Diamond Springs. With her father gone, her sister, Kristie, away at college and Sharyn living on her own, her mother had very little to occupy her time. Thank goodness she was still seeing Caison Talbot!

That was another case of a wedding that didn't happen. The only people Sharyn knew who made it to the altar were Ed and Trudy. Maybe there was something to be said for eloping and not planning something more elaborate.

She got out of the shower and brushed her dark red curls into rough order. She'd let her hair grow some from its shorter, clipped look over the spring and summer. Lots of hikes with Nick had given her a nice tan that blended well with her freckles. She opened her blue eyes wide and stared at herself in the mirror. Should she start using some kind of face cream? She was thirty this year and tiny wrinkles were appearing at the sides of her eyes and lips.

She slathered on some Oil of Olay her mother gave her for her birthday with the admonishment, "If you want to look your best as you're aging, you have to take care of yourself." It made her feel like a woman in a television commercial, but if there was one thing her mother knew how to do besides iron and cook, it was look good. Sharyn hoped she looked as good as her mother thirty years from now.

There was a knock on her door as she was buttoning her brown sheriff's uniform shirt. Even though she dropped thirty pounds, the uniform was still ugly and looked bad on her. Her hairstylist pointed out that her square jaw seemed squarer when she wore it. But it went well with her grandfather's WWII service revolver and gave her the sense of authority she needed to do the job.

She tucked the shirt into her pants and padded to the door barefoot. "Nick! What are you doing here?"

He walked past her and slumped down in one of the arm-chairs in her tiny living room. "I was thinking about murder and breakfast. You immediately popped into my mind. I can't think of anyone else I can talk to about my job while we eat."

She glanced at the chicken clock on her kitchen wall. "I don't have much time."

"This isn't a social call, Sheriff. Or at least we can pre-tend it's not. I'm here as the medical examiner for Montgomery County and all the little towns that includes. I have important information for you about the flying boat."

"As flattered as I am by being first in your thoughts with food and death, shouldn't you be having breakfast with Roy? The flying boat isn't part of my turf anymore."

He laid his head back on the chair. "I don't want to look at Roy's face this early in the morning. Cut me some slack, Sharyn. Bring your power bar if you want to. I can eat break-fast for both of us."

"I could make you breakfast here," she offered.

"I don't think so. I don't have to look in your fridge to know there's no food in there." He smiled at her. "And no offense, you're the best sheriff I've ever known, but you're also the worst cook."

"Such flattery before seven A.M." She sighed and put one hand across her forehead. "You'll turn my head, sir. How can I resist such a wonderful invitation to breakfast?"

He got slowly to his feet and came to stand in front of her. "You know, without your boots, I'm taller than you." He kissed the tip of her nose. "Now that I've said that, get your boots on and let's go eat something."

"Yes, sir, Mr. Medical Examiner." She saluted him. "Can I put on my gun too?"

His eyebrows rose suggestively. "Only if I can watch."

She laughed and went into the bedroom to finish dressing.

* * *

"So you lured me here with mocha and toast," Sharyn said while they waited for their food. "What about the murder?"

"I don't have a lot yet, but I have the name of the dead man." Nick sipped his coffee and paused dramatically.

"And you aren't going to make me ask you for it because this isn't my case and you're doing this out of the goodness of your heart, right?"

"Something like that. His name is Gunther Mabry. He's got a record. Mostly petty stuff; car theft, bad checks, stolen credit cards. He was shot with a Glock ten-millimeter at fairly close range. Probably from the back of the boat where Trudy's purse was. I think he walked back that way before he fell overboard. The blood got all over everything as he moved. Megan found some hair and blood on the backside of the boat. We think that's where he fell off."

The waitress brought Sharyn's dry toast and Nick's omelet, toast, bacon and pancakes. Sharyn waited impatiently until she was gone. "I remember him now! He's Duke's head mechanic. We questioned him while we were investigating Ben's death. Gunther Mabry must have kidnapped Trudy."

Nick picked up his fork. "Have we decided it was a kidnapping after all? The last time I heard, she walked out. I think that was *my* conclusion."

"I know that's what it *looks* like," she agreed. "But we both know things aren't always what they seem. Especially in a murder investigation. Don't jump to any conclusions you share with Roy until they've been checked out."

"Is the sheriff's department going to take the information and investigate, then give the results to the police department? Is that how it works?"

She leaned towards him. "You *know* this is different. Trudy is a member of the sheriff's department. The murder case may officially be Roy's but I have a vested interest."

"Which is why I'm here. But the county pays me to come up with conclusions. Even if they're ones *you* don't like. There was GSR on Trudy's purse. Her fingerprints were all over the boat. When I checked gun permits, Trudy has a ten-millimeter Glock registered to her. What other conclusion would you like me to take from that?"

Sharyn sipped her coffee. "I don't know yet. Do you have to give Roy those facts right away?"

"How long would you like me to withhold those kinds of facts from *you* on a murder case? I love you, Sharyn. But this is my job. I'm pretty good at it. I didn't want to find this evidence. I don't have any choice but to turn it over to Roy today."

"I know." She took a deep breath. "I'm sorry. You're right. I hate for Trudy to be accused of a murder she didn't commit. Especially when we don't know if she's alive or dead. Was any of that blood hers on the boat?"

"I don't know yet. There was a registration and a wallet in the glove box. They both belonged to the boat's owner, Duke Beatty, not Mabry."

"Not surprising. How could Mabry afford a cigarette boat like that on a mechanic's salary?"

"It'll probably take a few days to process the blood and the other fingerprints we found. I didn't finish the autopsy on Mabry yet either. Maybe we'll find out he drowned."

"You don't have to talk down to me. We both know how he died."

Nick finished his meal while Sharyn ate her toast and drank her coffee. "Will you tell Ed about this?"

"Maybe not yet." She wiped her mouth with a napkin. "We spent the rest of the night after the accident at his house going over everything again. We might have found something we missed before."

"What was that?"

She told him about the articles taped to the wall in the pantry. "I think Trudy might have thought Duke was involved in Ben's death."

"I saw that when I was there," he recalled. "I didn't think anything of it. Sports fanatics do that kind of thing. I have a whole wall about hockey players in my bedroom closet."

She didn't believe him. "You do *not*! If you have anything like that, it has something to do with guns. But anyway, thanks for sharing that info with me about Mabry. It doesn't bring me any closer to finding Trudy right now but it gives us all a heads up when we *do* find her."

"I'm sorry I can't do more to help. I don't know what we'll do without her."

"She's not dead," she corrected. "I believe that."

He took her hand in his. His dark eyes were serious. "We both know the odds get greater with every hour that goes by. You may never find her. I hope you're ready for that."

She swallowed hard. "As ready as I'll ever be. I think we might pay Duke a little visit and see what's going on out there."

"It's not your case, Sharyn," he reminded her. "Roy won't like you following up a lead on his first murder case."

"I know." She brushed toast crumbs from her hands. "But I can't sit around and do nothing. Besides, it could pertain to Trudy's disappearance, which *is* my case."

They walked out of the diner together. It was still cool and damp from the rain the night before. Diamond Mountain, the tallest in the surrounding Uwharries, was swirled with white mist. Traffic picked up as cars made their way towards the Interstate. Most of the new residents in Diamond Springs came for the peaceful beauty but they still worked in Charlotte and Raleigh.

"Be careful. I'll call you if I hear anything." Nick tucked a copper curl behind her ear.

"I'll count the minutes." She grinned up at him and put on her hat.

"How am I supposed to kiss you good-bye with that on?"

"Work around it."

He obliged her by sweeping off the hat with his hand and kissing her for several minutes while Diamond Springs looked on. A few cars honked their horns and walkers applauded as they passed them. When he was finished, he put the hat back on her head. "I'll see you later."

Her face was suffused with color. "I'm looking forward to it."

They walked off in different directions. Nick went a few

blocks down to the morgue under the hospital. Sharyn went across the street to the basement under the courthouse.

"Hey! Sharyn!" Jill Madison greeted her at the door to her office. "That was quite a smooch on the sidewalk. You're getting braver."

Sharyn took off her hat and hung it on the wall. As she touched it, she thought about Nick and smiled. "Hi, Jill. How's it going?"

"You don't want to talk about it. That's cool. Lucky for you nobody from the *Gazette* saw it or you'd be front page this afternoon."

"What brings you in?" Sharyn asked her, still refusing to discuss her relationship with Nick.

"A man from the shelter was arrested last night for breaking and entering in Harmony. I thought you might be able to help me out with that."

"I'll see what I can do. Who's the arresting deputy?" Sharyn picked up the mail on her desk. Coffee was made and messages were stacked. There was no sign of Ernie but she knew her head deputy had been there.

"Marvella Honeycutt." Jill read from her copy of the arrest warrant. "She's a little overzealous, isn't she?"

Coming from Jill, the poster child for the overzealous attorneys of the world, that was funny. Her fall from grace on a drug charge earlier this year was a long one. Sharyn managed to keep a straight face. "I'm sure Deputy Honeycutt was only doing her job."

"Maybe. But it seems to me she picks up quite a few homeless people from the shelter." Jill glanced at her notes. "Maybe she has a problem with the homeless."

"Would you like to file charges against her?"

"No. Not yet anyway." Jill laughed nervously. "You know, it's kind of weird knowing so much about the law but not being able to practice it."

"When can you appeal your suspension?"

"Not until next year. But I'm working on it. And thanks to you, I have my kids one Sunday a month. They were really happy to see me. All we did was knock around the lake and eat lunch at McDonalds, but it was nice. I didn't take them to the shelter. I don't want them to know I live there. One step at a time, right?"

"That's it," Sharyn agreed. They both knew Jill would never have her old life back again. Too much happened after she offered to investigate Senator Jack Winter. Sharyn was very conscious of the fact that Jill did it to help her.

Nightshift deputies Marvella Honeycutt, JP Santiago and Joe Landers came in from the street. Joe was a veteran deputy with over twenty years in the department. He offered an extra hand on the nightshift until their newest deputy could be trained on days.

"It's good to see you looking so fine, Sharyn." Marvella's dark eyes winked. "No wonder Nick couldn't keep his hands off you on the street."

JP laughed. "We heard it on the radio, Sheriff. Joe says you should be more careful or people will think you're fast."

Joe didn't take off his dark glasses, as usual. He handed Sharyn the patrol reports for the night. "Don't forget *easy* too, JP. Let's not let her get away with anything."

Sharyn ignored the teasing. She was used to it. Not immune, but slowly getting accustomed. "Deputy Honeycutt, Ms. Madison is here about a man you arrested last night."

Marvella's dark face grew fierce. "It must be another homeless person. I swear, she can't protect them all. Why don't they stay here in Diamond Springs and do their thing? That way Roy and his boys would have to handle it."

Jill walked up to her. "You can't go around looking for homeless people to harass."

Marvella held up her manicured hand. Her fingernails were teal blue. It was her only attempt to irritate Ernie with her non-conformity . . . this week. "I'm not harassing anybody, honey. If they do the crime, they gonna do the time." She moved her hand into position to slap JP's.

JP grinned and shook her hand. His broad Hispanic features showed the pleasure their relationship gave him even if his response to Marvella's high five left something to be desired.

"I'm heading home," Joe told Sharyn. "I'll be glad when I'm back on days. This is messing up my weekends with the 'guard."

"Thanks, Joe," she responded. "We should have Terry ready in another two weeks."

"Great. Have you heard anything about Trudy?"

They all looked at the empty desk at the front of the office. Calls were being routed through an answering service until they got Trudy back or replaced her. No one wanted to think about that yet.

"Nothing yet." There wasn't enough good news to bother with, and the bad news would only keep him awake. "I'll let you know if anything comes up."

The phone rang through on Sharyn's private line. Marvella and Jill started bickering as Ernie, Ed and Terry walked into the office. She answered the phone. Ernie would handle the problem between Marvella and Jill.

"We found Trudy's cell phone," Nick told her without preliminary. "It was in Gunther Mabry's pocket. It's older. No GPS chip. That's why you couldn't find it."

Trudy's cell had been a hot topic of debate. They knew it was gone but weren't able to triangulate a location for it. It was like it vanished. "Thanks. At least that's one piece of the puzzle."

"According to a police report, Duke Beatty said his cigarette boat was stolen three days ago. The same night Trudy went missing. Go get him!"

Chapter Three

Sharyn and Ed got out of her Jeep at the Stag-Inn-Doe. If possible, the nightclub was more rundown than ever before. The sunlight was harsh on the old wood façade. It stood right on the county line, making it difficult to prosecute the current owner, legendary racecar driver Duke Beatty. But the place had been an eyesore and a problem to law enforcement in both counties for almost fifty years.

The problem was everyone visited the place at one time or another. Some more discreetly than others. Every graduating high school class of Diamond Springs had a good-bye party there before heading to the beach. Despite drug deals and fights, the Stag-Inn-Doe managed to sail on. Nothing seemed to bother the rustic, ramshackle hut.

"It looks quiet." It was one of the few times Sharyn had seen the parking lot empty and the dismal shack quiet.

Ed grabbed his riot stick. "Let's shake things up."

"We're not going to find Trudy by knocking Duke in the head." She put her hand on his arm. "I know you're upset. If you can't handle it, you can wait out here. If we're lucky enough to find something we can arrest Duke on and close this place, I'm not going to lose a conviction because you were careless."

"If he's hurt Trudy I'll kill him, and you won't have to worry about it."

His normally carefree blue eyes were sincere enough. She believed him. She wished she'd brought Ernie with her. But he was so friendly with Duke, even looked up to him, she didn't want that either. Terry Bartlett, the new man, had been with the Diamond Springs police department only a few weeks before he made the move to the sheriff's office earlier that year. She was afraid he didn't have the experience to handle the case. Ed was going to have to do. He was too well trained to let this get the better of him.

"We don't know for sure what's happened," she reminded him. "Right now, this is all speculation. We're not in the movies, Ed. We have to take this one step at a time. I can't believe I have to say this to you. You have more experience than I do."

"Then don't say it." He walked past her and kicked open the door to the building. It stayed upright, swinging by a bolt. He looked back at her, his face rough with three days' growth of beard and a deep anger boiling in his soul. "Coming, Sheriff?"

Before she could send him back to the office, Marti Martin, the nightclub's manager, looked out at them through the new aperture. "What's going on, Sheriff?"

Ed grabbed the greasy little man by the throat and threw him down on the gravel in the parking lot. "Where's my wife, you little worm?"

Sharyn stopped him. "Go wait in the Jeep, Deputy."

"He knows where Trudy is." Ed drew back his stick to hit the squirming man on the ground. "And he's going to tell me."

"Not like this." She snatched the riot stick from his hand, wishing she'd realized what kind of shape he was in before they left the office. She was so used to his normally easy good humor, she didn't see it. She held her ground when he took a step toward her. "I'm not kidding, Ed. I'll suspend you until this is over. We aren't going to do it this way."

The man she'd called Uncle Ed as a child glared at her. "Sharyn, I won't argue with you about this. You don't understand. You don't know what it's like. I won't hurt him if he tells me where she is. All I want is the truth."

"Get back in the Jeep. I'll take care of this."

He put his hand on the stick and tugged. "Let it go, Sharyn! I don't want to hurt you!"

She used his anger and lack of balance against him. He pulled harder at the stick until she released it. When he took a step back, she kicked his left foot out from under him. He fell hard on the damp ground. Before he could look up, she had her knee in his back, holding him down.

"I'm sorry, Ed. But you're not helping Trudy this way. I don't want to do this. I shouldn't have brought you out here."

Eyes that normally laughed at her with a laid back sense of humor flashed with anger. "Don't do this, Sharyn. We've known each other all of your life. Your daddy would understand. He'd let me take care of it. We can't go back from here unless you let me up."

Marti laughed in relief, but didn't quite dare to get up. "Oh, I get it. This is some kind of extreme good cop/bad cop thing, right?"

Both uniformed officers turned their heads and yelled, "Shut up!" Marti put his arms across his face and kept still.

Sharyn radioed for help, not moving off of Ed's back. "I'm doing this for your own good. You're not yourself."

"And some day I'll look back and say thanks?" he snarled. "I don't think so. If you won't let me help, I'll quit. I swear I will. Trudy means more to me than this stupid uniform."

"Ernie?" she said into the radio, ignoring Ed. "I need backup out here at the Stag. Where are you?"

Before Ernie could answer, Ed flipped Sharyn off of his back. Marti made a high pitched squealing sound and ran inside the nightclub.

She was on her feet in an instant, wiping the red clay from her face and hands. The smell from the good earth was revolting, mixed with years of things she didn't want to think about. Her uniform was covered in it.

Ed stared at her. "I trusted you to help me find Trudy. I can see I'll have to go it alone."

"The only place you're going is home." She called for backup again. "You need to take a few days off."

"The only thing I need to do is find my wife."

Sharyn had never seen him this way. He was always so cool in every circumstance. He never took anything seriously. She could hear a siren coming towards them from a distance. Thank goodness Ernie was close by. "Stay where you are, Ed, please! Don't make me throw you in jail. I've always respected you. I know you're a good man and I don't want to lose you as a deputy. Let us take care of this. We'll find Trudy."

Ernie and Terry pulled up in a brown and tan sheriff's car. Gravel shot out from under the tires as the car came to an abrupt halt with the blue lights still flashing on the roof. "What's going on out here?" Ernie jumped out of the car. "I expected trouble. But not this." He stared at his two friends confronting each other.

"Take him home," Sharyn said. "Talk some sense into him. I don't want to see him in uniform again until he's had some sleep and knows what he's doing."

"Are you suspending him?" Ernie asked her.

"Three days. He lost it here. We can't trust him on the street until he's in better shape. I'm sorry, Ed. You know I wouldn't do this if I didn't have to. Stay home until we find Trudy."

Ed's face was full of disbelief and fury as Ernie put his hand on his arm. He jerked away from his old friend and fishing companion. "You don't have to bother suspending me, Sheriff Howard." He tossed his badge and gun on the ground at her feet. "I quit. Consider this my resignation. You don't have to worry about me messing up your perfect world again!"

Sharyn nodded, not trusting herself to speak. It all happened so quickly. She wanted to think she'd done what she had to but maybe there was some other way. Maybe she reacted too strongly. Ed was more than a deputy. He was a friend. He worked with her father before her. He taught her to dance. But she couldn't back down now. "Terry, come with me."

Deputy Terry Bartlett was only too happy to comply. He hurried to her side like a large puppy.

She looked down at the gun and badge in the dirt. When she looked up again, Ernie and Ed were in the squad car. A minute later, they were gone. Sighing, she picked up the gun and badge and took them to the Jeep. She could only hope Ed would get over being angry and see that she did what she had to do. She turned to Terry, who was watching the events with a look of total astonishment on his youthful face. "Let's go in."

"Are you really suspending Deputy Robinson?" He ran his hand across his closely shaved head. The short brown stubble didn't move.

"No," she answered. "He quit. Concentrate on what we're doing, Deputy. I don't think anyone else is here except for Marti. I think he's harmless. But let's keep our eyes open in case I'm wrong. This can be a hazardous place."

"Yes, ma'am." He took up a stance directly behind her as she walked inside. His hand rested on the pistol at his hip, like a gunfighter.

The Stag-Inn-Doe's interior was even worse than the decaying exterior. It was too dark to see much of it but the smell spoke for itself. A long, dirty bar greeted patrons as they walked in. The mirror behind it may have been new fifty years ago when the place was built. Now it was clouded with age and corroded with filth. To the left of the open door was a dance floor where live bands played on the weekends. To the right were tables and booths. In the back were small, private rooms that could be rented out for whatever anyone had in mind.

"Marti?" Sharyn called out. "I want to talk to you."

His head came up from behind the bar. "Is he gone?"

"Yes. But we're still here. Where's Duke?"

"I'm not sure. He's gone. He left late last night."

"How do you get in touch with him?" She picked up an expensive bottle of bourbon from the bar.

"I don't." His glance skittered across her face. "He comes in when he feels like it. I just run the place. I don't ask too many questions. You know what I mean?"

She smiled at him. "What if there's an accident?" The bourbon bottle smashed against the side of the bar. The stench of too many long nights and drunken parties was overshadowed by the sudden powerful scent of Jack Daniels. "What then?"

He bit his fingernail. "I don't know. He doesn't tell me anything. I only work for him, Sheriff. Ask him what you want to know. Haven't I always cooperated with you?"

She looked at Terry. "I think an accident might be about to happen in the storage shed. Deputy, look for the most expensive case of liquor back there."

Terry pulled out his pistol. "Yes, ma'am."

Marti glanced back and forth between them. "Wait! He'll kill me if that Courvoisier gets wasted. Maybe I know how to get in touch with him."

"Okay." Sharyn stopped Terry. "How do you get in touch with him?"

"I don't have his cell phone number or anything. He only gives that to girls he likes. But I think he's out at the track testing a new engine this morning. You can't tell him I told you. He'd kill me. And I mean that, Sheriff. He's not the man people like to pretend he is. He's mean and vicious."

Terry put his gun away at a nod from Sharyn. He folded his arms across his muscular chest and glared at Marti.

As effects went, it was pretty powerful. Terry was tall and well built. He looked like a poster for the Marines. Sharyn was pleased with his performance. He made up for his lack of experience with intuition. She liked that. "The speedway, right?"

Marti put his hands on his temples and closed his eyes. "I thought you and I wouldn't have so many run-ins after the motel burned down, Sheriff. I thought I was out of this routine with Duke up front."

"Get a real job, Marti," she advised. "Don't work for people like Duke. Then you and I won't see each other at all. There are ten thousand people in Montgomery County who don't even know what I look like. You could be one of those people."

"I'd do it if I could," he whined. "But I keep getting sucked into the jobs that pay more money. It's not like I want trouble. It just seems to follow me."

"Then we're bound to see more of each other." She handed him what was left of the bourbon bottle. "If I can't find Duke, I'll be back."

Terry was silent until they walked outside. He pushed the splintered door back in place. It leaned a little to the right but went well with the weathered façade. "That was cool!"

Sharyn got in the Jeep and fastened her seatbelt, waiting until he joined her before she said, "That wasn't cool. That was *desperate*. We're not ever supposed to be that desperate."

"I know I don't have a lot of experience, Sheriff, but you got what you needed without messing him up." He grinned. "It was *cool*."

"Okay. Thanks." He had a long way to go. She started the engine and pulled out of the parking lot. She called back to the office to let Cari know where they were going. Her computer savvy deputy was manning the phones unless an emergency came up and they needed her on the street. In her tenure as sheriff, Sharyn had hired an additional four deputies yet it still didn't seem to be enough. Her father made do with Ed, Ernie, Joe and Roy for twenty years.

"So you think Duke kidnapped Trudy?" Terry asked as she put down the phone. "Why would he do that? Do you think they had a thing going on?"

"No, I don't think they had a thing going on." She turned on the Interstate entrance ramp. "And don't say that in front of Ed. I don't know what their connection is yet. If there's any connection at all." She explained about the newspaper clippings in Trudy's pantry. "I think she was trying to find out something more about her husband being killed. But this is probably a long shot."

"Didn't Ernie say you investigated her husband's death? Was there any sign of anything but an accident?"

Sharyn considered the question. It was a valid one. After years of rehashing her father's and even her grandfather's cases, it seemed to be her turn. Did she make a mistake checking out Ben's death? Was she so eager to pin it on Jack Winter that she overlooked other possibilities? "At the time, we were all sure the ex-DA was involved in some way. There's been a lot of dirty politics and backroom deals in this town."

"You mean Senator Winter? What made you think that?"

She told him about the horses Jack owned. "It's not like Jack to let something like that go without some retribution."

"But now it might be Duke who was responsible." Terry shook his head. "This is a tough job. What will happen if you were wrong back then?"

She shrugged. "No one requires the sheriff to be right all the time. I suppose if enough voters don't like it, they won't vote for me. But it's not like I broke any laws that would force the commission to suspend me. I did the best I could at the time."

They reached the speedway. The new sign was still being installed. It had always been the Diamond Springs Speedway but the owners recently sold the name to a tool manufacturer that had recently moved into the county. Now it was the Tools America Speedway. The company was spending a fortune upgrading the old track. They were hoping to become part of the NASCAR short track circuit.

The security guard at the front gate waved his hands to stop them. "Anything I can do to help you, Sheriff?"

"I'm looking for Duke Beatty. Have you seen him today?"

The man nodded. "He's on the track with his crew checking out a new engine. Just follow the signs to the team parking area. You can walk in from there. Your backup is already here."

"My backup?"

"Your other deputy. He got here a few minutes ago."

She nodded to him, wondering if Ernie had the same idea. "Thanks."

Terry whistled through his teeth and put on his hat. "Taking down the Duke would be a major bust."

"Let's try to keep an open mind. We don't really have any evidence against Duke. Trudy's purse in his boat gives us a reason to question him. It doesn't mean he was involved in anything that's happened to her. As far as we know, she walked out of her house on her own two feet. She took her cell phone and her camera. That doesn't suggest a kidnapping."

"But the dead guy in the boat suggests something." He checked his pistol then put it away. "Something doesn't feel right here, does it, Sheriff?"

Another drama queen. Sharyn sighed. Maybe that was why the chief didn't put up more of a struggle when Terry decided to leave. "We're about to find out, Deputy. Just remember, we're *investigating*. We don't know what happened yet. We don't want to jump to conclusions."

"You mean like you did with Trudy's husband?"

"That's what I mean. Let me do the talking for now. You keep your eyes open and listen so we don't miss anything else." She parked in the lot at the west side of the racetrack. There was no sign of another car. Maybe Ernie was parked in another lot since he got there first. She put on her hat and adjusted her holster.

They locked up and followed the signs to the pit areas. The sound of a car running wide open on the track grew louder as they got closer. Even with only one car circling, the high sides reflected the noise back in on them. A group of men in blue coveralls were standing together, watching the car with binoculars. One of them was wearing earphones and talking to the driver.

"Sheriff." A tall man with a large wrench nodded to her, raising his voice to be heard above the sound of the car.

"I'm looking for Duke Beatty!" she yelled back. "Is he in the car?"

"That's right. What do you want him for?"

"Ask him to come in," she instructed. "I need to talk to him."

Another man stepped forward. "I'm Spunky Tucker, Duke's crew chief." He shook her hand. "Can I help you, Sheriff?"

"Sorry. Only Duke can help me. Ask him to stop."

Spunky smiled, dark glasses hiding his eyes. His thin lips barely formed an irritated curve. "He's testing an engine. Whatever you have to say can wait a few, can't it?"

"No. I'm afraid not. He can finish testing after I talk to him."

"Sheriff, isn't that a little harsh? I mean, what can be *that* important?"

She considered the question. "Murder? Going to prison for life or worse. I don't want to ask again, Mr. Tucker. Have Duke stop the car."

Tucker nodded and spoke to the man with the headphones before he turned back to her. "He should be coming in now."

"Thanks." She shaded her eyes from the bright sun and the brilliant blue sky to watch the red and yellow race car coming down the track. The crack of gunfire broke the monotonous sound of the engine. The man in the headphones started shouting. Tucker demanded to know what was wrong even as the car spun out of control and crashed into the concrete side wall. It flipped three times before ending up on its roof in the grassy middle of the track.

Duke's crew ran toward the car, fire extinguishers in their hands. Smoke drifted up from the wreck as Sharyn had Terry call 911. She ran toward the left of the track where the sound of the gunfire seemed to originate. It looked to her like someone shot Duke.

"I can't believe we were here when someone took out the Duke," Terry gushed as he followed her.

"Draw your weapon, Deputy, and keep your head down!" Sharyn did the same as she spoke. She put her back against the side of the concrete building. The signs outside showed directions for the speedway offices. There was one door leading into the track area, but no sign of the shooter. "Cari," she spoke quietly into her radio, "get everyone out here. There's been a shooting."

"Yes, ma'am," Cari responded. "Anyone hurt?"

"I think Duke Beatty's been shot. Terry and I are fine. We're going in where the shot seemed to come from. It's the office complex on the east side of the track."

"Wait for backup, Sheriff!"

But Sharyn switched off her radio. "I'll take the right," she explained to Terry, "you take the left."

"But shouldn't we wait for backup? Ernie says always call it in and wait for backup."

"That's only if you're not with me."

Terry still seemed uncertain, but Sharyn was pushing open the door. He had no choice but to follow her lead.

She kicked open the weathered wooden door. She could hear movement to the right, behind a high counter. She rushed in with her revolver drawn and her head down. "Stop right there!" There was a man bending over a rifle on the dirty green tile floor. Terry came up beside her and leveled his pistol in the same direction. "Come up nice and easy with both your hands locked behind your head."

The man came up slowly, his hands behind his head. His broad shoulders stretched the red flannel shirt he wore. His blue jeans were clean, a crease down the legs. His blond curly hair was tousled.

"Ed?" Sharyn asked in disbelief. "Is that you?"

He started to turn around. Terry moved quickly, knocking him down on the floor. In thirty seconds, he had the suspect subdued and cuffed. Grinning broadly, he turned back to Sharyn. "That might be a record. Do you all keep track of your fastest times?"

"No," she growled. "Get off of him." She pushed Terry aside and helped her suspended deputy to his feet.

Ed scowled. "I don't know about a record for fastest time, but this must be a record for a deputy getting knocked down twice in the same day by his friends."

Sharyn freed him. "What are you doing here? Didn't I tell you to go home?"

Before he could answer, there was a noise from the next room. In unison, all three officers drew their weapons and confronted the person stumbling into the main body of the office.

"Trudy!" Ed yelled and ran to her. He lifted her in his arms and cradled her against his body. "I thought you were dead."

Trudy blinked her eyes and looked around her. "Where are we? What happened?"

"Call another ambulance," Sharyn said to Terry. "Call Ernie and see what's taking him so long. I need people outside the track. No press allowed in until we figure out what's going on."

"Yes, ma'am."

Ed didn't let Trudy go. They held each other until Sharyn suggested they sit down. Even then, he kept his arm around his wife.

Sharyn handed Trudy a cup of water and sat on the other side of her. "Where have you been? What happened to you?"

Trudy shook her head as she drank the water. "I don't know. Everything is so hazy. Maybe I got hit in the head or something. I don't feel very well."

"Never mind, honey." Ed helped her lie down across a few chairs. He stroked her brown curls. "EMS people will be here soon. They'll take care of you."

Sharyn frowned, sorry she was so worried about Trudy that she didn't give her time to recover. She was just so happy to see her. And so anxious to know the whole story.

"Sheriff?" Terry called from the other side of the counter. "There's something you should see."

Leaving the couple alone, Sharyn went around the counter and walked over to look at the rifle on the floor. "That must be the rifle that shot Duke."

"It says property of Montgomery County Sheriff's Department," Terry whispered.

Her mouth became a tight line as she peered closer. "It's Ed's rifle. See that mark right there?" She pointed to a white indentation in the stock. "Ed did that running after a suspect last year. I was there with him." *And could testify this is his rifle.* The realization came unbidden, unwelcome. Ed didn't shoot Duke. It looked bad right now. But there was a reasonable explanation. There had to be.

"Should I leave it here or pick it up and put it in his car?" Terry crouched down beside it like it was a snake.

"There's every reason to believe it could be involved in this shooting." She hated the words, had to force them from her mouth. "Leave everything where it is until forensics gets here. We have to be careful. If we investigate one of our own, we have to be sure there's no hint of impropriety."

"What are you saying, Sharyn?" Ed came up in time to hear her words. "You think I shot Duke?"

"You were pretty angry back at the Stag," Terry remarked.

Ed's gaze didn't move from Sharyn's face. "Are you telling me I'm under suspicion for this?"

She stood up. "Just stay over there with Trudy for now. Let us sift through this and try to figure it out."

"I don't care about that," he answered. "I'm asking if *you* think I'm guilty of shooting Duke?"

"No, of course not!" Her voice and gaze didn't waiver. "I don't believe you'd shoot anybody because you were mad."

"Thanks. I can handle the rest."

Sharyn turned back to Terry. "Watch the door from the hall. No one except our people or forensics comes in. Understand?"

But before she could do the same with the door from the track, Spunky Tucker and another member of Duke's pit crew ran in. "He's dead," Tucker told her. "Duke's dead. Somebody was a mighty good shot. They hit him in the head even though he was traveling over a hundred miles an hour."

"I've called the medical examiner and the paramedics," Sharyn explained. "They should be here soon. Don't touch anything."

"We had to drag him out of the car," the young man with Tucker told her. "We were afraid the car might catch on fire."

"That's fine. We just need to keep the scene as intact as we can. Did the camera get what happened?"

"We had a spotter filming it from the roof for performance checks." Tucker glanced at the rifle on the floor. "Is that what killed him?"

"We don't know yet. But I'll keep you apprised." The sound of approaching sirens broke up their conversation.

"Maybe you should call Duke's family so they don't have to hear about this on the news."

Tucker agreed. "Did you see anyone, Sheriff? Any idea who did this?"

"Not yet. We'll know more when the ME gets here."

Ernie and Cari came in, and were shocked to see Trudy. Then Cari escorted the crew members back outside as she got Terry to help her take statements from everyone at the track.

"What happened?" Ernie whispered to Sharyn as he watched Ed and Trudy hugging each other. "What's Ed doing here?"

"Did you drop him off at their house?"

"Yeah. What made him think about coming here?"

"I don't know, Ernie. Terry and I came in and saw Ed either putting the rifle on the floor or about to pick it up. I can't be sure which. The only thing I know for certain is that this is his rifle and he was threatening Marti at the Stag earlier. He knew we were looking for Duke. He's been desperate to find Trudy. She walked out of that other office like she'd been asleep."

Ernie rubbed his face. "What now? We have to take him in, don't we?"

She agreed reluctantly. The paramedics were finally there. Ed lifted Trudy on the stretcher and kissed her cheek. She held his hand as they checked her vital signs.

"Let's keep this quiet for now," Sharyn said. "Let the press pick up on Duke. Maybe we can get some answers before they focus on who did it. You take Ed back to the office. Make sure he stays there. I'll see what we can find out here and wait for Nick."

"All right," Ernie said. "But be careful. If anyone thinks we're giving Ed special treatment, they'll be on us like a bunch of angry hornets."

Ed joined them after the paramedics took Trudy to the hospital. "They think she might be a little dehydrated but nothing serious. I can't believe it. I didn't know if I'd used up too many favors to get her back."

"You're still on that lucky streak," Ernie congratulated him. "Now let's get you out of here until we can find out what really happened. 'Cause I know you, old son. You couldn't hit a horse from ten feet away with that rifle."

Ed laughed. "It'll be okay. I'm not worried about it."

Sharyn walked with Ernie and Ed into the team parking lot. She paused at the door. Joe and Marvella came too late to stop reporters from gaining entrance to the lot. But they were kept out of the office building and the track. Nick was navigating his way through the crowd when the press saw Sharyn and surged towards the door, shouting questions as they came.

"Is Duke really dead, Sheriff?"

"Have you ID'd the shooter, Sheriff?"

She didn't think anything of Ed pausing beside her. They didn't want to make a scene or give the press any indication that everything wasn't exactly as it should be. Ernie took a step toward him but didn't try to restrain him.

"I did it!" Ed shouted to the reporters. "I killed Duke Beatty!"

Chapter Four

"That was the stupidest thing I ever saw anyone do." Ernie pushed Ed into the back of the squad car. "What in the world were you thinking?"

Ed shrugged, his arms pulled behind him by the hand-cuffs they were forced to put on him in front of the press. "Did you think I'd stand there and let them blame Trudy? It's bad enough they might want her for killing that boy in the boat. If I can figure out some way to take the blame for that too, I will. We all know she didn't kill anyone."

"I can't believe you've been in law enforcement for all these years and you don't know better." Ernie shook his head in disgust.

"I won't let you arrest Trudy for this," Ed promised. "I'm the right suspect. I was angry and abusive with Marti at the Stag. He'll testify to that. I went home, ignored my suspension. I brought the squad car here, took out my rifle."

"You're a moron!" Ernie pushed him again.

"Can you take him back and put him in a holding cell without hitting him?" Sharyn asked as she closed the car door. "Or should I have Terry take him?"

"I'll take him." Ernie smacked the side of the brown car. "But he's *still* an idiot!"

"Don't let anyone else talk to him," she said. "Get him inside and keep him quiet."

Nick stood by as Ernie left with Ed. "Did Ed just confess to murder?"

"Yes." Sharyn wondered if she could go back to bed and get up on a better side later. Where did this day go so wrong? "He was probably on TV too. He was 'saving' Trudy."

"What happened?" Nick asked as they walked back to the track through the main gate.

She filled him in as they moved through the slanting rays of fitful sunshine—more clouds were already starting to move in. The smell of gasoline from the wrecked car was still strong as she sniffed the air. "It's crazy. I know Trudy wasn't involved with this. You could see she was barely conscious. But I know Ed didn't do it either. We need some real answers before people start coming up with their own."

"I'd better get this processed fast then." He glanced up at the sky. "It looks like rain again. We barely got finished with the boat last night before it started pouring."

The number six race car was still on its side in the grass. Terry and Cari ushered everyone away from the site. Reporters and onlookers, including Duke's racing team, were being kept in the press room beside the offices. It was odd to be on the track and not hear any noise at all. The faint drone from a small plane overhead emphasized the unusual quiet.

"Megan and Keith are late again."

"I'd fire them if I could get anyone besides two interested grad students to take the job for the money I'm paying them," Nick said. "Especially now that I have to beg the county for a new van."

"I thought you and Julia Richmond had a *special* relationship," she teased. "Can't she sweet talk the rest of the county commission into giving you the money?"

"I don't want to get into that." He opened his kit and took out a pair of gloves. "I'm dating the sheriff, you know. She's got a quick temper. I'd hate for her to shoot Julia." He knelt down beside Duke's body on the grass. "I suppose they had to move him out of the car."

"Not every crime scene can be exactly like you want it." She looked at the broken body of the Diamond Springs' legend, his red and yellow jumpsuit covered in blood and dirt. His face was almost unrecognizable. "They were worried about the car catching on fire. At least you didn't have to deal with *that*."

"Somebody was a good shot." Nick found the single bullet hole in Duke's head. "They must've targeted the windshield as he came around. He was hit almost right between the eyes. Death would have been instantaneous. Blood spatter, the wound and body temperature look like they'll confirm that he was killed in the car in the last hour, not before."

Sharyn looked back at the office where she found Trudy and Ed. "Ed's a good shot but he's not an expert marksman."

"I'm not sure that will help since he told everyone he's guilty. Besides, a good shot can be a marksman with a little luck and the right wind."

She agreed with him. It would take more than that to save Ed. She'd have to find whoever pulled the trigger. There had to be a connection between the two murders. What were the odds of two different people killing Duke and his mechanic in the last twenty-four hours? It seemed to her Duke had finally crossed the wrong person.

If Ed wouldn't have intervened, Trudy would've woken up accused of both homicides. Someone managed to put her right in the middle of two crime scenes. They couldn't have known Ed would be there too. But why choose Trudy? Was she just available and snooping in the wrong places?

"Where did you say you found the rifle?" Nick finished the preliminary exam on Duke and took pictures of the car and the dead icon.

"It was on the floor in the office over there. I'll take you over when you're ready to go."

He looked around on the grass and the section of track closest to the car. "I don't see much going on out here. The bullet came through the windshield and struck Duke in the face. No exit wound. It should still be in there. I'll have the car towed to the impound lot. But I think everything we're looking for must be around the office."

"Okay." They started toward the gray office building. "Anything else yet on Gunther?"

"Not yet. I had three tests to give and a visiting college dignitary to amuse, besides another call to *another* crime scene." He glanced around the empty track. "Where were you when all this happened?"

She explained that she was out there to question Duke about the boat and the dead man. "I was hoping he might have some answers about Trudy."

"I probably shouldn't tell you this," Nick began, "but since the cases overlap, I'm willing to make an exception. Trudy's fingerprints are on everything in that boat, *including* Gunther."

Sharyn wasn't surprised. "I'd say somebody wanted to get Duke out of the way and they were looking for a convenient scapegoat. Trudy disappears. Duke's head mechanic is found dead in a boat Duke owned. Trudy's pocketbook is in the boat. The bullet that killed him probably came from Trudy's gun. Duke is shot by Ed's rifle with Trudy in the next room."

"Enter Trudy Robinson," he suggested. "Maybe someone wants the Stag-Inn-Doe. I think that's the way Duke got it."

"I suppose I can see why they'd kill Duke for a piece of property." Sharyn opened the office door for him. "But why Mabry? He's just the mechanic. And why bother framing Trudy for it?"

Nick paused at the doorway and took out his fingerprint kit. "I don't know. I'm not good at puzzles like you are. Is the rifle still here?"

She brought out the gun that was bagged and tagged. "No doubt it's Ed's rifle. He said it's been missing a few days but he didn't report it. He thought it would turn up."

"But doesn't that clash with your theory about Trudy being set up?" he asked, crouching by the door. "Why didn't the killer stalk Duke with Trudy's Glock and shoot him, unless he or she wanted to set Ed up too?"

"That does kind of spoil the effect," she admitted, glancing at the ground close to where he was working. The sun glinted off a small object in the red dirt. She leaned down and picked it up using a tissue from the desk. "What's this?"

"Something you shouldn't be touching without your gloves on? That's just a guess." He used his fingers to follow along the gray wall until he reached the small window that overlooked the track. "Pretty neat. Whoever shot Duke cut a hole in the window first."

Sharyn put the round circle of glass into the plastic bag he held open. "I guess the shooter thought the rifle barrel would be harder to see than a whole person standing outside shooting at Duke. They had a video camera recording the car today. Chances are they would've got the shooter too."

"I can testify that Ed didn't do the crime," Nick pledged. "I can see him whipping out the rifle and killing Duke but not cutting a hole in a piece of glass to do it. If he thought the rifle should stick out of the window, he'd just break the glass."

"That's true. Probably not enough to get him off but you're right."

"Didn't Ed or Trudy see anything?"

"Trudy wasn't awake until I got in here. And I don't know about Ed since all he can do is take the blame for Trudy."

"That makes it tough." Nick examined the window pane. "I see the hole in the window and I saw the glass circle outside. What I don't see is the glass cutter. Did you find that yet?"

"No." She looked outside again. "I don't see one. Maybe the killer took it with him."

"I'll have the kids check it out. They'll have to go over the whole office anyway. We'll check whatever prints we find, but I don't expect to find much."

"I know what you mean. Whoever did this was careful and methodical. No doubt he or she wore gloves."

"Which wouldn't protect him or her from GSR. As soon as I get done here, I'll test Ed and Trudy for it. Maybe that will help prove their innocence."

"Thanks." She leaned over and kissed him. "I'm going

back to Diamond Springs. I'll feel better when we can start making some sense of this. How are you for dinner tonight?"

"I can be free if you can. But we should probably go out since I'll have to head right back to the morgue."

"Sounds like fun to me." Sharyn paused in the doorway. "Let me know if you find anything unusual. And try to keep my case separate from Roy's. I know how you like to tell everybody what's going on in other cases."

He laughed. "Get out of here. I'll talk to you later."

Sharyn parked the Jeep in the parking lot behind the courthouse. She found Ernie sitting beside Ed in a temporary holding cell they used when they were waiting to transfer a prisoner to the county jail. "This looks like fun. Did anyone order lunch?"

Ernie got up and opened the cell door. "I wish you'd try to talk some sense into him. He's making up ways he shot Duke. The boy's lost it. He belongs in a place where they can take care of him."

"Maybe." She ignored Ed. "But Joe told me if Ed doesn't change his story before he gets here, he's going to use some new martial arts technique he learned in his last combat training simulation."

"You can both stop talking about me like I'm not here," Ed protested. "And there isn't anything Joe knows that can make me change my story. I killed Duke. Trudy didn't. That's it."

"Okay." She rested her hip against the bars. "Tell me how you did it."

"What's to tell? He was driving the car. I grabbed my rifle. I went outside and shot him." Ed glanced at Ernie. "Lucky shot."

"I think so," Ernie said. "Last time we were at the firing range together, you had a hard time hitting a stationary target much less one moving that fast."

Sharyn didn't tell Ed about the window at the racetrack office. It was better for him to keep his version of the story without her tainting it. "Thank you, Deputy. We'll let you know when we need more from you."

"What about Trudy?" Ed demanded. "How is she?"

She locked the cell door when Ernie was out. "They were still examining her on my way back. I'll let you know. Lunch should be here soon. I hear it's not too bad. Better than they have at state prison in Raleigh anyway."

"You can't expect me to put decent food above Trudy." Ed hung his head. "You know she's the best thing that ever happened to me. And Ernie would do the same thing for Annie. You'd do the same for Nick."

Sharyn covered his hand that rested between the bars. "You're probably right. But don't worry. We're going to find out who killed Duke and Gunther. That way you and Trudy can *both* stay out of jail."

Ed squeezed her hand, his blue eyes intent on hers. "Thanks. But if not, I'm going to admit that I killed Mabry too. I'll agree to admission and waive trial. Nobody will want Trudy if they can have me that way."

"Then you better come up with a good story," she advised. "A better one than you just gave me about Duke." The guard rolled up with the lunch trays. "I'll talk to you later. But do us both a favor and don't admit to anything else until we've had a chance to check this out. I don't want to lose you, Ed."

Ernie shook Ed's hand through the bars. "Sorry if I roughed you up, old son. You know I love you like a brother."

Ed smacked himself in the head. "So *that's* why you were an only child! Don't worry about it. Sharyn was a lot tougher this morning."

Sharyn and Ernie left the holding cell and walked back towards the sheriff's office. Roy met them in the hall. "Where's my suspect, Sheriff?"

Ernie took a step toward him but Sharyn held him back. "If you're talking about Trudy, she's at the hospital. I think she was drugged."

The chief hitched up his pants and adjusted his hat. "Okay. I'll question her there. *Then* I'll bring her in."

Sharyn took a deep breath to steady her voice and help

her find something to say besides threatening him if he went near Trudy. He had a murder case where the only evidence was a woman's pocketbook. The same woman had a gun registered to her that was possibly the murder weapon. She'd bring that woman in as well. Just because it was Trudy didn't matter. "I know it looks bad for her, Chief. But you know her too. You worked with her while you were a sheriff's deputy. You *know* she didn't kill anyone. This was set up for her to take the fall."

"I don't know anything at this point, Sheriff. But I know a suspect when I see one. Trudy was on that boat. If we find her gun and the bullet matches the one in my dead man, you know I'll have to arrest her for this crime. Nobody likes to prosecute family. But isn't that what you're doing with Ed?"

Ernie pushed Sharyn's restraining hand out of the way. He stood almost nose-to-nose with Roy. His thin, whipcord strong body was a direct contrast to the chief's corpulent frame. "Don't even start to think that Trudy or Ed is guilty of these murders. You have to do your job. I'll grant you that. But don't let me hear of you stepping over any lines of conduct with Trudy or I'll—"

"Nice to see both branches of our local law enforcement getting along so well." Eldeon Percy, Montgomery County District Attorney, greeted the two men. "Good morning, Sheriff Howard. Sorry to hear about your unfortunate turn of events. Naturally, the state *could* be brought in to investigate this matter, if you can't handle it. No one would expect you to try and find evidence against your own family."

Ernie took a step back from Roy. "There's nothing to investigate, sir. Ed's been with this department for a long time. If anything, we owe him an investigation into proving his *innocence*."

Mr. Percy shifted his alligator briefcase from one hand to another. His white suit was carefully cleaned and pressed as always. His tall, elegant form and piercing blue eyes were a familiar sight in the courthouse. "Deputy Watkins, I know this is hard for you. It's hard for all of us. But I heard Deputy Robinson confess on the radio. There's not much left to say.

He's thrown away his career. Be careful you don't do the same."

Sharyn watched Ernie bite his lip to keep from saying anything else. Instead, he nodded respectfully and walked away. Roy did the same, leaving her with Mr. Percy.

"Keep me apprised of the situation, Sheriff. Your best bet now would be to let those state boys figure this out. This could look very bad for you. Watch your step. Many others will be watching everything you do."

She didn't reply. He nodded at her and walked up the stairs toward the wing of the courthouse that held his offices. Nothing Percy ever did was threatening or beyond the bounds of good behavior, unlike his predecessor, Jack Winter. Yet she always came away with the feeling those cold blue eyes might freeze a person's soul. There were so many dark recesses behind his smile that she didn't want to consider what the man was like who hid there.

When she reached the makeshift sheriff's office in the old basement boiler room, she found Ernie sitting at his desk, staring at the ugly green wall. Two volunteers were answering the phone and a few highway patrolmen stopped in to file a report on an accident. Deputy Cari Long was taking their report while both men flirted with her. Sharyn focused on Ernie, dragging him into the tiny area they'd set aside for a conference and interrogation room.

"Roy's right," Ernie told her when she closed the door. "So is Mr. Percy. Ed hanged himself out to dry by making that admission for the reporters. There's nothing we can do to help him."

Sharyn drew a rickety ladder-back chair to the folding table. "That's stupid. More stupid than what Ed did. At least I can understand *his* reasoning. He wanted to save Trudy. Who are you trying to save with that attitude?"

"It doesn't matter. He's going to jail. You and I both know it."

"I don't know anything of the kind. I think we need to find something else to talk about."

"Like what?"

"Who wanted to set Trudy up to take the fall for these two murders?" She paced the tiny amount of floor space. "Someone purposely lured her into this situation to cover up killing two people. They held out the bait and when she took it, they pulled her in. Dad always admired a good fisherman because he said they had to have patience and the right bait."

Ernie's mustache twitched. He ran his hand through the sprig of brown hair on top of his head. "Good point, Sheriff. Now all we have to do is resign from our jobs and start our own private investigating firm. Because you know that's the *only* way we're going to be able to prove any of that."

"But you have to admit, it's the truth. The FBI might come and investigate what we're doing. It doesn't matter. Ed and Trudy don't have to be my friends for me to do my job. That includes finding out what happened and why it happened. When we do that, Ed's confession won't mean anything. Especially since he was under duress."

"You're right, I suppose," he admitted. "I'm having trouble keeping myself objective right now. I know we can prove Ed and Trudy are innocent if we keep our heads."

Sharyn took the seat opposite him. "We don't have to be objective, Ernie. I wasn't when they were looking at you for murder. We know how to do our jobs. That's all that matters."

He smiled at her. "You're a good sheriff, in case I haven't mentioned that in a while. And you're right. Let's do our jobs."

When they stepped out of the small room, Cari hailed Sharyn. "Reporters have been calling here all morning. Are we going to hire someone else to answer these phones? If not, shouldn't someone with less seniority have to do it?"

Marvella ran down the steps into the office. "I just heard the news. Don't even tell me Ed killed someone. I won't believe it. I'll work double shifts or whatever else I have to do to prove it didn't happen."

"The only thing that's going to save Ed is finding the truth," Sharyn told her. "I appreciate your offer. But right now, I don't know what to tell you. When we have a plan and some leads, there might be something you can do. Until then, I need you on nights to keep things going."

Marvella twisted her bright pink scarf in her hands. "Whatever you need, honey. You know I'm here. Can I see Ed?"

"I don't see why not. But remember he's a prisoner right now. Don't do anything to break the rules. The FBI might be looking into this too."

"I'll be careful," Marvella agreed.

"You could take these phones for a while," Cari told her. "I have other things I should be doing. Right, Sheriff?"

"I'd love to help." Marvella grinned at her, her handsome dark face full of concern. "But you look like you're doing just fine, Cari. And the sheriff needs me at night. Right, Sheriff?"

"Until further notice, you're on the phones, Cari." Sharyn sorted through the problem quickly. "Marvella, go home and get some sleep. I might have to pull Joe from nights and let Terry pick up from you and JP."

Cari groaned as she answered another phone call. Marvella winked at Ernie as she saw him admiring her shiny pink shoes.

Ernie groaned and looked away. He couldn't say anything since she wasn't in uniform. "We're not gonna get jack out of Ed while he thinks he's protecting Trudy."

"You're right. Why don't we see what Trudy can tell us? There must be something she remembers. Something made her go to the Stag."

Ernie picked up his gun and his hat. "We're at the hospital, Cari. Don't forward any calls unless they're important."

"I wish I was at the hospital," she replied. "One man has called me three times this morning about a squirrel on his roof: What am I supposed to say to him? He wants a deputy to investigate. He thinks the squirrel is spying on him. How does Trudy handle things like this?"

Sharyn adjusted her revolver in its holster. "Tell him we'll send animal control out. Then call Bruce and Sam. Have them check it out."

"You're so good at this," Cari enthused. "Maybe *you* should be here."

"Nice try." Sharyn laughed. "But that's not going to happen.

Don't worry about the reporters and don't tell them anything. Take messages unless it's something really important. If we hear from the SBI or they come in, call me right away."

"All right. But my talents are wasted here."

"She's right," Ernie agreed with Cari as soon as they were out of earshot. "We're going to have to replace Trudy, at least temporarily. We need Cari out on the street. Even if you bring Joe in from nightshift, it'll be hard for us to handle everything."

Sharyn opened the driver's side door to the Jeep. "I know. But we have to make do. If I put Terry on nights, Marvella and JP should be able to get him through his training."

"I swear if Terry comes in wanting to wear a red bandanna or the like, I'm going to choke Marvella. What is it with her? I think we should have her tested for an authority problem."

"She was great at Sweet Potato Mountain. You should've seen her. I'd take her with me anywhere, in any situation. She saved some lives up there, Ernie. Whatever's wrong with her is something to do with you. You're the only authority she has a problem with. Leave her alone for a while. She's a good deputy. I think she just likes to see you get all flustered."

He glanced out the side window. "Flustered? Brides get flustered. I don't get flustered. I'm the lead deputy in this office. I enforce the rules and keep things going for you. Marvella likes to give me a hard time. When are you going to see that?"

Sharyn laughed. "Probably the next time you wear a pink scarf to work. Lighten up! She's only giving you a headache because you have no sense of humor with her. Try it some time. You might be surprised."

They pulled up in the Diamond Springs hospital parking lot. Ernie got out and slammed his door shut. "Can we concentrate on getting Ed and Trudy out of trouble?"

"You brought it up," she reminded him, locking the Jeep. The dark clouds that had been rolling in all morning began releasing their heavy burden of rain. "I hope Nick is done at the speedway," Ernie said.

"I hope so too." Sharyn walked quickly into the warm shelter of the hospital. "He said there wasn't much outside anyway."

They asked about Trudy at the receptionist's desk and were directed to the third floor. Sharyn was surprised to find her ex-deputy, David Matthews, standing guard outside the room. "David. The chief got you over here pretty quickly."

He stood in the doorway and didn't smile. "Sheriff. You know Trudy's *our* prisoner."

"That's hard to say," Sharyn argued. "We think she killed Duke too. Ed came in after the fact. We need to question her."

"I'll have to ask the chief." David took out his cell phone. "That's good news about Uncle Ed though. My mom has been after me for information since she heard his confession on the radio."

"You know Trudy too," Ernie pointed out. "Having her charged with both murders won't be any better."

"Well, that's true. But it's not as bad as Uncle Ed being charged." David spoke briefly with the chief. "He says you can go in."

"Thanks." Sharyn nodded at him as she slipped by into the room.

"Like he was gonna stop us," Ernie growled.

"Easy. We're in a tricky position here. We might need to have the chief on our side to figure this out. Let's not alienate him already."

Trudy was sitting up in the hospital bed. She was looking out the window as the rain drenched Diamond Springs. When she saw Ernie and Sharyn, she started crying. They both rushed to her side to comfort her.

"I know it was stupid," she began blurting out, "I know I should have told you all." She punched the hard bed. "But, darn it, I wanted to solve it myself. You're always going out, taking care of business. It's always answer the phone, Trudy. Take care of the office, Trudy. We need you here, Trudy. No one ever cares that I want to have an adventure sometimes. I want some of the danger and excitement you have."

Sharyn and Ernie listened to Trudy sob between her ramblings about danger and excitement. Ernie shrugged at the questioning look in Sharyn's eyes. He patted Trudy's shoulder awkwardly. "It's okay, honey. We're gonna take care of you. You're safe now."

Trudy stopped crying long enough to throw his hand away from her. "You just don't get it do you? I don't *want* you to take care of me. I don't *want* to be safe. I've been safe my whole life. First with Ben and now with Ed. I've watched you go out every day, knowing your life was on the line. What have I done? Filed some papers. Answered the phone. I'm good, safe Trudy. You don't know me at all."

Ernie stared at her like he'd never seen her before. He put his hands in his pockets and didn't come close to the bed again.

Sharyn sat down on the edge of the bed and faced the woman she'd helped sort papers on the days she visited her father at the office. "Start at the beginning, Trudy. We need to know exactly what happened and what you remember if we're going to help you and Ed."

Trudy's brown eyes fastened on Sharyn's face. "What do you mean? Where *is* Ed? Why didn't he come with you?"

"He confessed to murdering Duke Beatty," Sharyn answered. "He's going to confess to murdering Gunther Mabry."

"Why would he do such a thing?" Trudy demanded.

"Because you'll be charged with both murders if he doesn't. He's in a holding cell right now. He confessed in front of the media as soon as they took you to the hospital today."

Trudy bit her lip and scrubbed her hands across her eyes. "That's the stupidest thing I ever heard! What *is* wrong with that man?"

"That's exactly what I said." Ernie re-entered the fray. "But he's doing it to save you from your 'adventure.'"

"That's ridiculous! Why would I be charged with killing anyone?" Trudy's gaze bounced back and forth between Sharyn and Ernie.

"Because your pocketbook was found in a cigarette boat covered with Gunther Mabry's blood. His body was in the lake, shot by a ten-millimeter Glock," Sharyn calmly explained as she studied Trudy's pretty face. "You know who Gunther Mabry is, don't you?"

Trudy nodded her head, her dark brown curls dancing with the movement. "I know who he is all right, Sharyn. He's Duke's mechanic. And probably the man responsible for Ben's death."

Chapter Five

Sharyn took a deep breath. "Start from the beginning. Don't leave anything out."

Ernie drew up a chair. Trudy glanced at him as she laced her fingers together. "It started last year. I know you investigated Ben's death, Sharyn. But I felt like there were other things going on that you couldn't know about. I had to find out for myself."

Ernie rubbed his forehead. "Why didn't you say something? And don't give me that claptrap about wanting to defy death. You know we would've listened. We've known each other too long for that."

"That claptrap *is* the way I feel," Trudy defended. "I wanted to be out on the street like everyone else. So I started going to races by myself. I watched the newspaper and the sports channels for information on Duke. I'd hang around after the races and buy drinks for the pit crew. It was the only way I could think of to get the answers I needed."

"And you believed Duke killed Ben," Sharyn added.

"At first. Then I realized I was missing an important truth. We all did." Trudy smiled at her. "Duke didn't kill Ben. *Duke's* life was in danger. Ben was driving Duke's car the night he was killed. If Duke hadn't been drunk, he would've been dead instead of Ben."

Sharyn remembered checking out that lead. It went

63

nowhere. "We knew that. I can understand why you'd think Duke killed Ben. What happened that made you think Duke was a target?"

"Because there were several other times he was almost killed in the last two years since Ben died. Little things happened to him. Cut harnesses. Bad tires. An unexplained fire. I started thinking about who'd want to kill Duke. The problem was that *everyone* hated Duke."

Ernie objected. "Everyone *loved* Duke! He was a good friend to lots of people. He helped homeless people and kept drug addicts off the street. We won't see his like again."

Sharyn rolled her eyes. "Despite Ernie's hero worship, we know Duke was involved in more than a few illegal activities. We couldn't touch him because he was so careful. We could never catch him with his pants down."

Trudy patted Sharyn's hand. "I know you did the best you could. I had to spend months getting down and dirty in some of the grossest places I've ever seen. I did things that make me shudder when I think about them. Things you *couldn't* do as the sheriff."

"And what did you find?"

"That lots of people wanted Duke dead. There would've been a line to finish him off. But I was looking at the one particular escape he made that cost Ben his life. The name that kept on coming up was Gunther Mabry. I'm convinced he was responsible for the accident that night."

"You think Gunther hated Duke more than the others and had the opportunity?" Sharyn questioned. "I remember talking to him. He had an alibi that checked out that night. He hadn't even worked on the car in over a week when Ben was killed. The car had a test drive before the race. Why didn't the problem show up then?"

Trudy shook her head. "I'm not sure. But Gunther pretty much confessed to me that he was responsible for the wreck. He hated Duke. It was outside money that made him try to kill him."

"Outside money?" Ernie frowned. "You mean someone

paid him to do it. We checked that out too. We thought Jack Winter paid Gunther to kill Ben."

"Instead, someone paid Gunther to kill *Duke*. Ben's substitution was last minute. Duke was a pretty smart man. Slick, anyway. He knew what was happening. He let Ben drive his car because he suspected something was up. Gunther waited as long as he could before the race but it was too late to take it back when he found out Ben was behind the wheel."

"So you confronted Gunther," Sharyn said. "You told him what you knew and he threatened you. You shot him to defend yourself."

"Please!" Trudy held up one hand and smiled. "That man wanted me the way a 'possum wants a bologna sandwich. He would've done anything for me. I didn't need to confront him. Not that I *would* have. I've worked with the sheriff's office for twenty years. I planned to turn all my information in to you. Then I got a call from him Sunday night."

"That's why you went out to the Stag-Inn-Doe." Ernie nodded.

"Yes. He said he had some information for me. I got up and left Ed sleeping. I had to do it before. It's no big deal. He sleeps like the dead. When I got out there, the place was dark. I left my car and walked towards the building. That's the last thing I remember before waking up at the track."

"Gunther didn't give you any hint of what he knew?" Sharyn questioned.

"We talked about the man who hired him to kill Duke. Gunther didn't know I was Ben's wife. He thought I was some racetrack floozy. He was bragging about all the important people he knew. I think he heard from the person who wanted Duke dead. He would've told me all about it if I'd met him."

Sharyn got up from the bed and looked out the window as the rain and wind came down from the mountains in ever increasing fury. People walking by closed their umbrellas and bent into the wet wind. "You probably didn't meet him because someone knew what you were doing. That's why your pocketbook ended up in the boat with him. We haven't found your gun yet. Did you take it with you that night?"

"Always," Trudy assured her. "Didn't you find my car at the Stag?"

"No," Ernie answered. "It was parked out on the highway. We thought you broke down out there and took a ride with someone. Ed thought you were kidnapped from the house. He couldn't believe you'd sneak out like that."

Trudy stared at her plain gold wedding band, her hand resting on the stark white sheets. The smell of antiseptic and bleach was strong in the room. "You know I didn't do it to hurt anyone. I wanted to find out what happened to Ben. That's all. I thought I could do it alone."

Sharyn opened the window a little to let in the rain-sweetened air. Then she faced Trudy. "Right now, Roy wants you for murder. The boat Gunther was killed in came up from the lake into Diamond Springs. Your pocketbook is his only lead."

"I suppose she'd be *our* suspect too if Ed hadn't wandered up in time to take the blame for Duke's killing," Ernie despaired.

"I'm sorry," Trudy told them. "Will Roy arrest me?"

"I don't know yet," Sharyn answered. "If he does, Ed will confess and take judgment without trial."

"He can't!" Trudy's hands went to her suddenly pale face. "I won't let him. I'll confess to both murders myself."

Ernie took off his glasses and rubbed his eyes. "I fail to see where that will help matters any. This is a mess. I'll grant you that. But both of you confessing could just lead people to think you did it together."

"Ernie's right." Sharyn took Trudy's hand in hers. "Don't say anything. We'll get you a good lawyer, if we need to. But let us see what we can dig up. We know you didn't kill anyone. We just have to prove it."

Trudy hugged her. "I'm so sorry, Sharyn. I didn't mean to cause any trouble. But maybe if Roy doesn't arrest me, I can get out and be some help. I know the racetrack now. I know all the people involved. I was so close to catching whoever is behind this."

"I appreciate the offer," Sharyn said with a smile. "Let's worry about getting you out of here first. Then we'll talk."

"I can't believe you didn't shoot her down right then," Ernie said when they were in the hall. "How much worse would you like this to be? If Trudy gets out, we need to get a court order that makes her stay at home until we know what happened."

"That's the attitude that caused this trouble in the first place," Sharyn reprimanded him. "Can't you see how important this is to her? She didn't mean anything bad to happen. But if we don't let her help, she'll be out trying to solve other cases."

Ernie glared at a passing orderly. "It's stupid and risky. She'll probably get herself or one of us killed in the process. I guess we'll have to hope Roy has enough to arrest her for now."

"You mean so Ed will take the blame?"

"And then she'll take the blame for both murders." He shook his head. "Just shoot me right now. I don't think I can handle this much stupidity at one time."

"You have to." Sharyn pushed open the door outside and held it for him. "Trudy and Ed need us. We can't let them down."

They ran through the heavy rain and got in the Jeep. "Where do we go from here?" he wondered. "Now we know what happened to Trudy that night but I don't see where that helps."

"Up to a point we know what happened. We need a copy of Trudy's lab work when it comes in. My guess, since I didn't see any outer trauma, is that she was drugged. Whoever did it probably shot Gunther with her gun and put her stuff in the boat. They kept her around until the hit on Duke. Then they left her in the office with the rifle."

"Maybe we could go out and have Nick take a look at the Stag-Inn-Doe to see if there's any evidence she was there for the last few days," Ernie suggested. "I hate to do that to him. I can't imagine how bad it would be to do forensic work there."

Sharyn started the Jeep. "Yeah, I know. He'll be whining about it for a month. But that's a good idea. Maybe we could establish some kind of timeline on everything that happened. Even though we have Ed in custody, our investigation has to center on Trudy. The first thing we should do is go back and pay Marti another visit. If he inherited the Stag from Duke, he probably knows more than he's telling."

But Marti Martin was in the hasty process of packing when they got to the nightclub. "I know you don't think I'm sticking around and waiting for *my* turn."

Sharyn nodded and Ernie closed the battered suitcase Marti was packing. He put one hand on top for good measure. "What happened to Duke?"

"I don't know. You're the detective. You tell me. They say he was shot. I say if someone killed him while he was going around a track at over one hundred miles per hour, he was hit by a pro. I can't even *shoot* a gun without throwing up."

"And for some reason, you think that pro might come after you?" Sharyn asked.

"I don't know. I don't *want* to know. That's why I'm trying to leave. My motel was an independent business operation. I didn't have any partners." Marti picked up a few more shirts and stuffed them into a plastic bag.

"Duke had business partners?" Ernie picked up on his words. "Who were they?"

"Even if I *knew*, I wouldn't be stupid enough to tell you. I've stayed alive all these years by keeping my mouth shut. You can't pin these murders on me to save your buddies, Sheriff. And I'm not saying anything else."

Sharyn could see Marti was terrified. There was more he wasn't telling her. But he'd be gone as soon as they left. She had to bring him in with her. She could hold him as a material witness, possibly, *if* she could make the case before a judge. But without any evidence that something happened at the Stag, she knew a judge wouldn't hold him for long. Any evidence they might find against him later would be useless. "We're going to have to take you in, Marti."

"What for? I was nowhere near the track when Duke was killed. And I'm afraid of water so I don't go near boats. You don't have anything on me."

Sharyn took his arm. "I can hold you for forty-eight hours while forensics goes over this place. Something we find here might change your attitude. If not, I haven't lost anything and you can get out of town."

Marti's dark, weasel-like face twisted. "Come on, Sheriff. With everything that's happened here, it would be a miracle for anybody to find evidence on just one crime. Let me go. You don't know what you're messing with here."

"Tell me," she invited. "Then we might be able to get you to a safe house."

"You'll have to take me in," he promised, putting his hands behind his back. "At least everyone will know I kept my mouth shut."

Sharyn led him out to the Jeep. "Call Nick, Ernie and then let's find Marti a nice holding cell. Maybe he can bunk with Ed."

Marti protested loudly during the drive back to the courthouse. Sharyn reminded him that he could be free with a single statement. "Tell me who Duke's partners are."

"I'm not telling you anything. I want my lawyer. Then I'm going to sue you for wrongful persecution."

Ernie opened the cell door beside Ed. "Here you go. You should be nice and comfy inside. And you'll be safe as long as you don't get too near Ed's side."

"What's up?" Ed asked.

"Marti knows something about Trudy being kidnapped," Sharyn told him. "Don't hurt him. He's going to tell us what he knows."

Ed growled. "I won't hurt him. At least not where the bruises show." He clapped his hand on the smaller man's rounded shoulder. "I'm sorry about what happened before, Marti. You know I'd never do anything like that in here."

Marti moved away from him faster than seemed possible for his slug-like body. He grabbed the bars and stared at Sharyn. "You have to let me out of here. This isn't fair. You all are supposed to be the good guys. I want my lawyer."

"We haven't arrested you yet," Sharyn reminded him.

"I still want him."

"You give his number to the guard and he'll see you get to call him," Ernie explained. "I think you're in luck. You missed lunch but supper shouldn't be too long. I hear they make some good stewed beef here."

Sharyn and Ernie left Marti crying for justice from his cell. "You think he really knows something?" Ernie asked her.

"I don't know. He *did* say Duke had partners. Maybe you can check that out."

"Okay. I can check Duke's tax records, talk to some of his friends. What are you gonna do?"

"I'm going to see Spunky Tucker about those near death scrapes Trudy was talking about."

He opened the door for her. "Take Terry with you. He can still get out and learn a few things."

"I already sent him home. I don't want him out on the street tonight without any sleep. Joe's coming back tomorrow. I'll be fine on my own."

"A man was just shot out there," Ernie reminded her. "Take Cari. I'll answer the phones if I have to."

But when they got back to the office, there were plenty of volunteers running around the basement making coffee, answering the phone, and sorting the mail.

"I call it bringing in the troops." Cari grinned at them. "Anything new on Trudy and Ed yet?"

"Not yet, young 'un." Ernie scratched his head. "Where'd you find all these people?"

"In Trudy's emergency phone book." Cari looked at Sharyn. "Can I help now?"

"You've done such a great job setting this up," Sharyn answered, "I'm going to take you with me."

Cari grabbed her hat and gun. "I've been ready since I got here this morning."

"Be careful out there," Ernie warned again. "Keep your heads down."

"What's he worried about?" Cari asked Sharyn as they got into the Jeep.

"He's worried we might lose another deputy and he'll have to answer the phones or work with Marvella," Sharyn replied with a laugh. She started the Jeep and waved to Charlie, the impound lot caretaker, as they left.

Spunky Tucker was still wearing his dark sunglasses as he directed the number six car being loaded on the back of the rollback. The sides and top of the car were crushed but the cage that would have protected the driver was intact. Unfortunately, the shattered windshield and bright red blood stain on the driver's side told a different story. Duke didn't walk away from this one.

"Mr. Tucker," Sharyn addressed him, "I'd like a moment with you when you're finished."

"So now *you* can wait, huh Sheriff?" He didn't take his gaze off the car.

"I'm only trying to do my job, sir," she replied. "I'd like to ask you a few questions about Duke's driving record."

When the bright red and yellow car covered with expensive sponsor stickers was chained in place, he turned to her. "I don't know what I can tell you. Duke drove a race car for longer than you've been alive. He was in some close scrapes. No driver worth spit isn't."

He started walking toward the office. The yellow police tape cordoning off the area stopped him. "I still can't believe he's dead. Not like this. If he'd hit the wall and died, I wouldn't be surprised. But for some crazy deputy to shoot him dead—"

"I don't think my deputy killed Duke." Sharyn glanced up as the rain started coming down hard again. "Maybe there's somewhere else we can talk?"

"Follow me."

Tucker led the way through a side door that took them to one of the new luxury suites being built for fans to watch the race. Compared to the hard, open air seats that most of the fans were used to, this was an elegant and grand way to watch the race.

"Wow!" Cari's blue eyes grew rounder as she looked at the white sofas and fully stocked bar. Everything in the three-room suite was designed to make it a better experience watching the race through the eight-foot windows that over-looked the track.

"Three big screen TVs," Sharyn remarked, taking off her wet hat.

"It's a whole new world with these sponsors," Tucker told them. "This is where the big money is. Not out there on the thirty-dollar seats."

Sharyn noticed he still didn't take off his dark glasses. She ignored the fact and took out her notebook. "Trudy Robinson has been following up on some information that Duke's life was being threatened."

"You mean the woman who killed Gunther?" Tucker sat down on one of the white sofas, unmindful of his dirty over-alls. He spread his arms wide across the back. "She thought Duke was in trouble so she killed his mechanic, is that it?"

"Ms. Robinson was kidnapped, possibly by Duke and Gunther," Sharyn told him. "Is this *your* suite?"

"Nope. This one was for Duke. One of his new sponsors bought it for him. I guess he won't need it now." He smiled at her. "As for Duke kidnapping anyone, surely you know better, Sheriff. There wasn't another man more careful of his reputation than Duke. He wouldn't be involved in something that obvious. Gunther wasn't the kind to mastermind some-thing like that. He only did what Duke told him. So there you go. You can check it out. Anybody out here will tell you the same thing. Duke wasn't a fool. He knew where his bread was buttered."

Sharyn considered his words as she scribbled down some notes. She had to admit he was right from what she knew about Duke. When she threatened him once with a possible scandal involving a stripper who'd once worked for him, Duke was quick to help her find the answers she needed. He was too smart and too involved in his image to use it for anything except selling Cadillacs from his dealership. At least anything that a person would live to tell about. "The only thing that doesn't add up about that image is the Stag-Inn-Doe."

Tucker laughed and shifted one foot on his knee. "You know, everybody's gotta have an outlet somewhere. The Stag was Duke's outlet. It helped with his bad boy image too. On the track, you have to be a bad boy to win. Duke knew how to have everything. He was a winner."

"What about the accidents?" Sharyn revived her initial question. "Ms. Robinson believes someone was trying to kill Duke."

"Yeah," he muttered, "your crazy deputy."

"Let's say for the sake of this investigation that someone else was trying to kill Duke. If my deputy didn't do the job, who else might be interested in seeing Duke out of the picture?"

He shrugged. "Lots of people can't deal with a winner. They get jealous. They want him out of the way. But we've always known that. We're careful with Duke's cars. If Ms. Robinson thinks any of Duke's accidents were set up, she's wrong. Gunther was Duke's head mechanic for ten years. I've been his crew chief for longer than that. Nobody messed with those cars besides us."

Sharyn's blue eyes clashed with Tucker's behind his dark glasses. "And did you gain anything by Duke's death?"

"If you call unemployment gaining something," he quipped. "Duke's been my ride through this business, Sheriff. His death means I'm a fifty-one-year-old crew chief without a job. And all those other drivers who didn't like Duke sure aren't going to hire me."

"When was the last time you saw Gunther?" Sharyn continued.

"I see him every day close to a race. I probably saw him yesterday but I couldn't tell you when or where."

She closed her notebook. "Could I get a list of everyone else who works on Duke's cars?"

He nodded. "I'll have it faxed over to you. Anything else?"

"Did Duke ever mention his partner at the Stag-Inn-Doe?"

"I never heard mention of a partner. I think Duke owned the place himself." Tucker got to his feet. "If that's all, I should be going. Duke's racing team will still go on. I need to see about that."

Sharyn thanked him for his time then she and Cari walked out of the suite into the rainy afternoon. It was early yet but the rain made it seem later. Streetlights were coming on around them on the racetrack as they walked by Duke's damaged car still waiting to be taken to the impound lot.

"So you think Duke's partners at the Stag had something to do with this?" Cari asked.

"I don't know," Sharyn admitted. "But Marti seemed to think so. I doubt if we find them listed on the deed for the place or any other legal document. Duke was smart but shady. His partners are probably smarter and darker. My father always thought drugs and guns came through there. He couldn't prove it."

They paused to look at a huge yellow sticker shaped like a stag's head on the side of Duke's mangled car. Sharyn could feel someone's gaze burning a hole in her back. Spunky Tucker was standing in front of the luxury suite staring at them, his hands in his pockets. His sunglasses were finally put away. Her cell phone rang. "Sheriff Howard."

"I heard back from Trudy's doctor," Ernie told her. "She was drugged and dehydrated. The doctor thinks she was probably out of it for the last three days. He said it didn't look like she'd had anything to eat or drink for that long."

"Okay. That might help *her* case. It doesn't do anything for Ed."

"I talked to Nick about going over the Stag. He said he'd

get to it as fast as he can. He wasn't too happy about it. I'm getting ready to go home. Nothing yet on anyone who might be Duke's partner at the Stag. Did you find anything out there?"

"Nothing out here except some attitude from Tucker. What do we know about him, Ernie?"

"Nothing right now, but I can check him out. Have you got a feeling about him?"

Sharyn sighed. "Not really. He was standing next to me when Duke was killed and he seems to lose everything now that he's dead. All the same—"

"I'll check him out. I guess it will do Ed some good to cool his heels in jail overnight. I told Mr. Percy we weren't ready yet to formally charge him. It will buy us a few days anyway."

"Any word on the chief filing charges against Trudy?"

"Not yet. Probably not until tomorrow at least. She's supposed to be released from the hospital tomorrow morning. I expect Roy to make his move then."

"You're right," Sharyn replied. "I'm on my way back. Talk to you later."

"They really don't have much to hold Trudy," Cari remarked as they pulled out of the parking lot. "Ed's confession is better for us."

"Except he didn't do it," Sharyn reminded her. "But you're probably right about Trudy. Roy may not be able to make enough of a case to prosecute if he can't find a weapon. Trudy's rundown state and the drugs in her system work for her. In the meantime, I guess I'll talk to Caison about defending her. She needs someone like him on her side."

Sharyn dropped Cari off at the office without going inside. She had confidence that Marvella and JP could handle some of Terry's training starting that night. It's not the way she wanted it to be but she had to work with what she had. She glanced at her watch. She had enough time for a shower and a change of clothes before she met Nick for dinner. They'd probably go to that bar and grill next to the hospital where all the doctors hung out. It wasn't her favorite place, but it was fast. Nick had his hands full with the double homicide.

She parked on the street outside her apartment and went inside. While she was waiting for the hot water to come out of the cranky old water pipes, she took the code book she'd found six months ago out of its hiding place behind the medicine cabinet.

Sitting cross-legged on the bed, she looked through the ever increasing pile of notes and e-mails she'd amassed trying to decipher it. There were two college students working with her. One from the University of Indiana and the other from MIT. She didn't give them any personal information. Whatever was in the book was something her father wanted to hide. He may have been murdered for it.

She'd found it by chance as they were moving everything from the old sheriff's office, Roy's office now. It was hidden in a recess behind a painting of her father. She'd been trying to decode it ever since with an increasing sense of frustration.

They'd deciphered some numbers but nothing that made any sense. It was hard for her to believe her father had gone to such lengths to hide this information. He wasn't a secretive man. Whatever was in the little black book was important to him. She was certain it had something to do with his relationship with then Senator Caison Talbot and DA Jack Winter.

During her time as sheriff, she'd uncovered bits and pieces about the good old boy network that took in many other famous local names. She suspected there were deep undercurrents; drugs, guns, influence peddling between the men who ran the town and the county. The closest she'd come to any real answers was with one of the men convicted of killing her father telling her someone paid him to do it. He was killed in a prison fight before she could make a deal with him for the rest of the information.

She put away the book with a sigh and walked into the

shower before the hot water was gone. She didn't have time to work on the book then. She'd work on it as she always did, sometime between midnight and morning. Maybe that's why it was so slow moving. She only worked on it when her brain was close to shutting down. She believed the answers to her questions were in that book. She was just too busy with other issues to be able to spend more quality time with it.

She didn't tell anyone about the book. Not even Nick or Ernie. She worried that one of them might give it away. Not purposely, of course. Although sometimes Ernie seemed like he was holding back information about her father from her. With Nick, she was more worried about him being hurt because of what he knew. Jack Winter had sharp talons. She'd managed to avoid them but they'd ruined Caison's life so that Jack could have his senate seat. And they'd all but destroyed Jill Madison when she came too close to the truth.

After her shower, Sharyn brushed her hair, and put on some light makeup to cover a few of her freckles. She sprayed on some of the expensive perfume Nick got for her birthday. She looked at the turquoise shirt she wore with her black jeans. It wasn't fancy but they weren't going anyplace that it mattered. It was always a relief just to be out of her uniform.

Grabbing her pocketbook and a light jacket, she switched off the lights and opened the door.

"Sheriff Howard?" A short man in a plain brown suit addressed her. He flipped out a badge in a wallet. "Special Agent Gallagher, FBI. Do you have a moment?"

Chapter Six

"Of course." She stepped back into her apartment. She recognized the second agent with Gallagher. He presented a weapons demonstration at the disastrous law enforcement retreat on Sweet Potato Mountain over the summer. "Agent Brewster. Nice to see you again."

Brewster nodded. "Sheriff. Good to see you too."

"What brings you to Diamond Springs?" She watched the men walk into her kitchen, closing the door behind them. They were dressed almost identically in plain brown suits and white shirts. Only their ties gave them away. Brewster wore a gold-and-blue-striped tie. Gallagher's was flat brown. If she had to guess, she'd say it was an indication of their personalities.

"We're here about an ongoing investigation, Sheriff Howard," Gallagher began. "We've been monitoring Diamond Springs for several years. Suffice it to say, this area is a major conduit for drugs and guns. They pass through here between Charlotte and Raleigh. The connection has been here for years."

"Why wasn't I informed of your investigation?"

"Because there are some very highly placed individuals suspected of being part of this conduit," Gallagher answered. "We didn't want to come to you with any details until we had a chance to watch you in action."

"I've been sheriff for five years." She stared at him in open amazement. "It took you this long to watch me?"

Brewster shook his head as he stepped into the conversation. "There were never any doubts about your honesty, Sheriff. The bureau has a lot of irons in the fire over this one. Some officials were afraid of bringing another person in on this. We've misjudged a few in the past. We don't want to lose anyone else."

Sharyn sat down on one of her kitchen chairs, the truth hitting her midsection with a sickening blow. "My father?"

"Yes."

An enormous wave of relief swept over her, making her knees feel weak. All the fears she had about one day finding that her father wasn't the good guy she imagined were washed away. He was working with the FBI. He wasn't involved with Jack and Caison. The doubts she faced every time she looked at the black book weren't going to come true. Her father was innocent.

"I'm sorry we couldn't tell you sooner." Brewster sat beside her at the table. "I realize it's been a burden for you. But your father wasn't dirty. He was one of the most honest men I've ever known."

Sharyn smiled. "Thanks. With everything I've learned about things that have gone on in Diamond Springs, I could only hope he was on the right side."

"He was killed for it," Gallagher bluntly stated. "We warned him that he was too close. He wouldn't back down. As you almost learned, the two men you put in prison for his death were paid to kill him."

"How do you know?"

Gallagher shrugged. "We've been listening to your conversations since you became sheriff. We needed to know where we stood with you. Especially since your relationship with Caison Talbot and Senator Winter have been close and personal. Just like your father."

Sharyn understood what he meant. Caison's on again/off again relationship with her mother almost made him a member of her family. Jack frequently implied personally and to the press that they had a more intimate relationship. It wasn't true, but she could see what it might look like to an outsider. Even Nick half joked about it. "What made you decide to trust me now?"

Brewster sat forward in his chair, his eyes intent on her face. "You handled yourself well on the mountain over the summer. We've seen nothing but honesty and a desire to rid this area of its bad influence for the past five years."

"But your newest investigation has to stop." Gallagher got to the point. "It's threatening everything we've put together up to now."

Sharyn studied the two men while her brain worked overtime. "You're not asking me to back off a case that could put two innocent people in prison for crimes they didn't commit."

"That's exactly what we're *telling* you to do." Gallagher adjusted his tie, looking smugly superior.

Brewster added quickly, "We're so close. Killing Duke Beatty was a major move for our players. They've been setting it up for a while. Unfortunately, we don't have all of our ducks in a row yet. We need more time."

"How much more time?"

"We're not sure," he admitted. "But we need these people to feel safe a while longer. If they feel threatened by this turn of events, it could compromise all the work we've done."

"My people, my *friends*, are in jail. They'll go to trial and prison unless I bring the truth out. No investigation is worth that."

Gallagher put his fists on the wood table and glared at her. "Not even to finally face the people responsible for your father's death?"

Sharyn was caught in a whirl of emotions. Logic and truth vied with her need for revenge, her anger over her father's death. Still she couldn't let Trudy and Ed go to prison to pursue the cause so dear to her. Anger was her response. "Let me get this straight. You've been investigating this area for at least seven or eight years."

"That's right. I think you'll have to admit our investigation takes precedence over yours." Gallagher rocked back on his heels.

"What I have to admit," she replied in a quiet voice, "is my embarrassment at your level of incompetence. You want me to let my friends go to prison for an investigation you haven't been able to complete for years. If you say I've danced all around the truth and I haven't been looking at it with all of your facts, what have *you* been doing, Special Agent Gallagher?"

"I think a little healthy respect for your government might be in order, Sheriff Howard. But since that doesn't seem to be the case, let me rephrase. Let the investigation into Duke Beatty's death drop for now."

Sharyn lifted her chin and glared back at him. "No."

Brewster put himself between them. "We're not asking for another five years, Sheriff. We're only talking for a few days. A week at best. There's been movement in our investigation. We're finally going to be able to wrap this up. No small thanks to you and our informants."

"Informants?" She forced herself to relax. Basically, they were all on the same side. It might be better to find a way to work with them than to be ordered to comply. She could keep her own parameters that way.

"That's right," Brewster said. "We've had some people undercover in key positions. One man for several years. They've made a difference to the case. We've all worked too hard and lost too much not to see this through."

"A few days." Sharyn drew a deep breath. "A week at best."

"That's right," he promised. "How long will that be to your investigation? Not even enough time to do more than arraign your friends. You know they'll both make bond. Before they go to trial, this will be over."

"And they'll both be exonerated?" Sharyn wanted the terms spelled out. She wished she could get it in writing but she knew the best she could do was the agents' words. "Everyone will know who really killed Duke and his mechanic?"

"Not as if you have much choice in the matter," Gallagher retorted, "but, yes. Your friends will be in the clear."

"We'd appreciate any assistance you can give us." Brewster stepped in again to smooth the way between them.

It was one of the hardest things Sharyn ever agreed to. Especially because she realized she couldn't tell anyone. It would mean she'd have to look in the other direction while the people who believed in her, depended on her, were left without a clue. But she knew she didn't have a choice. "What do you want me to do?"

There was only one person Sharyn refused to keep in the dark about what was going on. After the agents left her, she took Ed out of his holding cell.

"What's up?" he asked as she looked at him and looked at her handcuffs. "It's okay. You can cuff me. It's the rules. And you never know who's watching."

Sharyn put the cuffs on him, leaving his hands in front. "Come with me. We have to talk."

They walked through the empty courthouse until they reached the DA's office. No one was there, but Sharyn had a key to get in. Neither one of them could bring themselves to sit behind Eldeon Percy's neat desk. They both took visitors' chairs and faced each other.

Sharyn explained everything the FBI told her about their investigation. Then she told him what they wanted her to do.

Ed nodded. His baby face was stubbly with a growth of blond-brown beard and his blue eyes were worried. "This is a mess, huh? I'm sorry I made it worse. I was just so worried about Trudy."

"Yeah. You picked a bad time to be a hero." She squeezed his arm.

"Like you wouldn't. You'd do the same thing. What happens to Trudy?"

"I don't think Roy will be able to develop a case against her. Her physical condition goes along with her account of what happened. And all he has is her pocketbook in the boat.

They haven't found the gun yet. Even if they do, I think it's a toss up about whether or not a judge will buy it. Mr. Percy doesn't like to prosecute *anyone* involved with law enforcement. But he has to do his job."

"And I sit in jail, hopefully waiting for trial?"

"No. I don't see any reason why you won't make bail. Especially with a good lawyer. Caison said he'd represent you."

"Unless I take back my confession and demand a trial." He bent his head as he considered the consequences.

"Yes." Sharyn put her hand on his. "We both know you didn't shoot Duke. But the FBI thinks they know who did. If you take back your confession, say you were crazed with worry about Trudy, it will buy us some time."

"And if I don't?"

"Then I'll keep investigating and the FBI will have to deal with it. I don't care what else is lost. It's up to you."

"Okay. I'll take back my confession. As long as Trudy is in the clear. If something happens that things don't go that way, I go back to taking the blame. Probably for both murders. I won't let her go to prison, Sharyn."

"I won't either," she promised. "I know I'm not supposed to be pushing the investigation on this case anymore but did anything happen with Marti after I dropped him off?"

"He made a call and a couple hours later, he had a visitor. I couldn't see who it was. But Marti was whistling when he came back."

"Thanks. I'll check on it."

Ed laughed. "Do you think you can figure out how *not* to investigate this case?"

"There's a first time for everything, right?"

"I suppose so. But I think you'll have to break your leg or go on vacation to look the other way. I know you, Sharyn. It's gonna be a lot harder for you than for me. I don't mind the time to catch up on my reading. And I like jail food. It's an orderly life, you know? If I wasn't a deputy, I probably would've ended up here."

She hugged him and laughed. "You're crazy, you know? But we'll get through this. I'll find a way to sneak Trudy in to see you. Get some rest."

"I will. Thanks." He got to his feet in one easy movement, his hands still cuffed. "I guess we should be getting back now. We don't want this to look too suspicious."

She walked him back to his cell then went to the registration book at the guard's desk. There were only three sign-ins that day. One of them was there to see Marti Martin. Jack Winter's broad signature was remarkable on the sheet. What had Marti said to him to bring the senator to the temporary lockup?

She wanted to ask, would've ferreted Jack out and demanded to know. But that would look like she was investigating. Probably not a good idea. It struck her that it could be equally suspicious if she simply sat back and let Ed stay in jail. Anyone who knew her would know something was wrong. That included Jack.

"Hello, Sheriff Howard." JP jumped up from his desk when he saw her walk into the sheriff's office. "What brings you here tonight?" His broad, smiling face looked pleased and apprehensive.

"I couldn't sleep," she lied. "It's quiet tonight, huh?"

"Yes. Marvella is out on patrol with Terry. I am answering the phone and taking other calls. But so far," he shrugged, "no other calls."

She smiled. After a long time of JP being so serious it was painful, he was finally lightening up. He'd always been a good deputy. But the more time they spent together, the less stiff and formal he became. "That's the way it is sometimes. I just stopped in for a minute. I'm late for dinner."

He glanced at his watch. "A *very* late dinner. It's almost midnight."

"You're right. I guess I'm going to do some apologizing with my dinner. Has Nick called here?"

"No. I checked on Ed. He was doing fine. Marvella wanted to know how you could let this happen. I told her you do the best you can." His dark eyes were serious again. "What are we going to do about Ed?"

Figuring this was only the first time she was going to hear that question, she said, "The best we can, JP. Like everything else. Say hello to Maria for me and give Luci a kiss. I bet she's growing fast."

"Si," he said then corrected, "Yes. She is as beautiful as her mother. I'll tell them you asked about them."

"Thanks. I'll talk to you later." Sharyn took out her cell phone as she was leaving the office. Nick wasn't picking up at home. Surely he wasn't still at the college. She tried there but there was no answer. Finally, she called the morgue.

"Yes?" his irritated voice shot out.

"Sorry I'm late. Are you still up for dinner?"

"Sorry, I've already eaten. Maybe next time."

Sharyn waited, heard him sigh. She smiled, picturing him with his black hair sticking up all over his head and a mean expression on his face.

"I lied. I haven't eaten." His voice was dark and angry. "Where have you been?"

"I'll tell you over dinner," she promised. "My treat."

"There's only one place open this time of night unless you want to drive to Wendy's out on the Interstate."

"I'll meet you at the diner."

"I was afraid of that."

Over greasy fries and stale coffee, Sharyn told Nick about picking up Marti Martin. She wanted to tell him about the information she got from the FBI but knew she couldn't. It made her want to sing it out in the street. Her father wasn't guilty of being part of the problem in Diamond Springs. He was trying to be the solution. Knowing he was killed for his part in it only brought vindication and a more solid need to bring the killers to justice.

"While you were out having a good time," Nick told her when she was finished, "I was finding evidence for your case. There were no unusual fingerprints on Ed's rifle. But I felt like that was a given from the beginning. There was a strange kind of red streak on the stock. I couldn't identify it so I sent it off to Raleigh. Megan swears it's lipstick."

"Lipstick? That's interesting. I suppose the bullet from the rifle matches the bullet you found in Duke?"

"I'm afraid so." He grimaced as he sipped his coffee. "But I tested the clothes Ed was wearing. There was no GSR on him. Unfortunately, I think there's a pretty good chance there wouldn't be any residue on whoever fired the rifle."

"How's that possible?" She paused with her french fry halfway to her lips.

"Because the window blocked it. The shooter had so much of the barrel outside the glass, I don't think any of it would've turned up on his or her clothes."

Sharyn sighed and put down the greasy french fry. What was she thinking eating it anyway? She wiped her fingers on a napkin. "So that doesn't really help Ed."

"Not really. I got Trudy's clothes from the hospital and Keith tested them. There was no GSR on her either. But there was some residue on her purse."

"I take it you've decided to keep me in the loop on what's going on with that case?"

Nick ate the fry she put down after dousing it with ketchup. "Only because this case is important to you too. It may even be a part of the case you're working. At least that's my story if anyone asks."

She smiled at him. "Thanks. Since you're in such a giving mood, what about Gunther? Have you found anything else about him?"

"He was shot in the back at close range. We don't have a weapon yet so Trudy is still in the clear. That was definitely his blood in the boat. From the pattern of bruises on his body and the places we found blood, I'd say he was piloting the boat. Someone came up behind him and shot him. Gunther tried to get at the person, lost control of the boat. He bounced from side to side trying to reach the back of the boat. He finally got back there but was thrown into the water. There's some massive damage to the hull. He may have hit something before the boat hit the dock. There wasn't any water in his lungs. He died of the gunshot wound before he could drown."

Sharyn digested his account of the death. "Anything about the killer?"

"He or she was shorter than Mabry," Nick answered. "Figuring the trajectory of the bullet, the person who shot him was pointing up. Mabry was about six inches taller than Trudy."

"Is that in your report?"

"Yes. They pay me to help solve the case for them. The fact that there's no gun is in Trudy's favor. So is the lack of GSR. She was still wearing the same clothes she left in Sunday night."

"Can I get a copy of the report?" she asked him.

"For twenty-nine dollars ninety-five plus tax, shipping and handling," he replied. "But only for a limited time."

Before Sharyn could tell him that he had a strange sense of humor, Jill Madison joined them. She slipped into the booth beside Sharyn, ate the last few fries and finished Sharyn's cold coffee. "Is this an important meeting between medical examiner and sheriff or a tender moment between lovers?"

"Hello, Jill." Nick folded his arms across his broad chest and sat back. "Have some fries."

"Thanks. But there aren't any left." Jill grinned at him, sweeping her shaggy blond hair back from her face. "Are you ordering more?"

"No," he said. "I'm going home."

"Don't let me run you off." She got to her feet and waited for him to move so she could sit down.

"Are you staying?" he asked Sharyn as he slid to the end of the booth.

"She's staying," Jill answered. "We have a lot to talk about. Right, Sharyn?"

"You don't have to go," Sharyn told him. "I'm sure whatever Jill has to say to me you can hear."

He put some money on the table for the bill. "I'm sure I could. But why would I want to?"

"Now you've hurt my feelings." Jill sniffed and scooted in to take his place. "Could we order more food, Sharyn? I'm still hungry."

"Order whatever you want." Sharyn got to her feet. "I'll be right back."

"What is it with her?" Nick asked as she walked him to the door. "And why is she always hanging around you?"

Sharyn never fully explained to him about what happened to Jill. She didn't want to involve him in the search for her father's killer. He knew about her trip to Raleigh to take a statement from Skeeter Johnson and about Skeeter's untimely death in prison. He didn't know about Jill's part in that or about Jill continuing to investigate Jack Winter until he set her up to be arrested on drug charges. She didn't plan on telling him tonight. "Jill's had a rough time," she defended. "I'd like to help her."

He put his hand on her shoulder and smiled into her eyes. "You can't help everyone, you know. There's only one of you."

"I know." She caressed his hand.

"Okay." He drew a deep breath. "That being said, I'm leaving. I know I can't stop you from trying to save the world. Just be careful."

"I will."

"I'll have that report on your desk in the morning."

"Thanks. Goodnight, Nick." She leaned close and kissed him softly on the lips. "I'll talk to you later."

"You bet."

When he was gone, she went back to sit across the booth from Jill, who was already eating another order of fries and slurping a Coke. "You guys are so cute together."

"Thanks." Sharyn tried not to look at the fries, feeling queasy.

"Any word on Trudy?"

"Not yet. I don't think there's enough evidence to hold her for the murder."

"Cool. How about Ed?"

"We found him at the track with the rifle that was used to

kill Duke. He took responsibility for the shooting. There's not much left to say."

Jill's eyes narrowed. "But you're still investigating, right? You don't think Ed killed Duke. You won't rest until you find out who did it. You're Sharyn Howard. That's what you do."

Sharyn realized that Jill's questions were not only valid but she should expect them from everyone. It *was* what she did. Everyone knew her well enough to realize she wouldn't sit still and wait until Ed went to prison. In promising the FBI not to investigate any further for a few days, she was facing an identity problem that could destroy everything. If she didn't at least pretend to be investigating, everyone would be suspicious.

"Thanks, Jill. You're right. I won't rest until Ed is out of jail."

"You're welcome. I knew you weren't thinking right about it or you would've seen it yourself."

A man walked into the diner and glanced around at the sparse number of people eating. He wore a movie-style, full-length black trench coat and heavy black biker boots.

Sharyn watched him check out the cash register and the waitress who was counting her tips. Unfortunately, with growth and progress came more crime. She knew this man was there to rob the diner. Most people would've thought twice about stealing from a restaurant frequented by large numbers of law enforcement, especially with the police and sheriff's offices right across the street. But someone from out of town might not know that. She carefully took out her revolver from the holster under her jacket and waited for him to make his move.

It happened suddenly. He flipped up the side of his coat at the same time that he demanded money from the waitress. Heads turned but no one moved. The waitress whimpered and opened up the cash register. She handed him the cash and checks from inside it.

"Is that all?" he growled. "That won't even cover my gas coming out here."

"That's it," the waitress said. "They deposit in the bank at eight. We don't do a lot of business after that."

"Fine. I'll take it." He glanced around the diner. "Everyone stay where you are. Pass your valuables to her. Give her your wallets."

Once the waitress was away from him, six of the twelve people eating in the diner stood up and leveled weapons at the robber's face. He drew out a crossbow from beneath his coat and faced them, until he felt another gun come to rest beside his ear.

"Let's put that down nice and easy," Sharyn told him. "As weapons go, that's pretty creative. Did you make that yourself?"

"I'm not answering any questions. I want my lawyer."

Roy and one of his officers, both with spaghetti stains on their shirts, took custody of him from Sharyn. "It's getting where a fella can't eat anymore without having to think about business."

"What is this?" the bowman demanded, finding himself surrounded by various members of law enforcement. "You guys having a convention or something?"

Roy turned the man's head so he could see out the plate glass window. "What does that say?"

"Diamond Springs Police," the would-be robber read aloud. "Oh, man."

"Let's get this boy locked up so we can all finish our supper," Roy said, nodding at Sharyn. "Guess we need some kind of sign outside that says we all eat here."

"I guess so." She put away her revolver.

"Thanks for your assistance, Sheriff." Roy wiped his mouth and shirt with a napkin. He glanced at Jill who was still dunking fries in ketchup. "My mama used to tell me a man was judged by the company he kept. Be careful."

She smiled. "My father always said don't judge a book by its cover. Guess we had much different parents, huh Chief?"

He grunted and turned away to finish eating. Sharyn put down a few dollars more on the table to cover what Jill ate. "I have to go. I'll see you later."

"Thanks, Sharyn." Jill slurped more coffee. "Good luck with your investigation."

Sharyn walked home slowly through the damp, cool

night. The lights on the lake gleamed up from the center of town. Black like the sky above it, the lake reflected the stars and the lights from the houses around it.

The streets were almost deserted, less so now than five years ago. New people brought a different lifestyle to the small community. A twenty-four-hour convenience store stood where a bait and tackle store had been for twenty years. An arcade was on Main Street in an old dime store. It was still open; red, green and purple neon lights flashing. She didn't always agree with the decisions the county commission made to allow new growth in the area. The arcade quickly became a hangout and people complained about the noise. The convenience store attracted its own share of problems.

The growth was in the county too. New subdivisions attracted thieves and scams. The big mall off of the Interstate brought in much needed revenue but demanded frequent patrols and developed problems with shoplifters and car thieves. The number of people and problems quickly outgrew even the newly focused sheriff's department. Right now, Sharyn was waiting for the county commission to okay funding for two new deputies. Though they didn't patrol the town of Diamond Springs anymore, her deputies were stretched too thin to be effective.

Shivering in the cooler night air, Sharyn let herself into her apartment. The wind from the lake was a barometer of the colder air coming down from the mountains. People were already mourning the loss of the warm weather and covering up their boats for the winter. There'd be some nice days left. Indian summer would come in October. But the trees would be stripped of their leaves by then. Aunt Selma would have all of her apples stored in jars as butter and sauce. Some things didn't change.

She didn't waste any time putting on brown shorts and a Montgomery County Sheriff's Department T-shirt. She sat down with renewed interest in the black code book. Her grandfather's revolver was still in her shoulder holster as she went online to chat with the two students who were helping her with the book. She couldn't tell them what the FBI told her but she did explain that they might be looking for a schedule of some sort.

She spent two hours online with them, throwing ideas back and forth about what the code could be and what it might be disguising. They signed off but Sharyn was still too pumped to go to bed. She got some Diet Coke from the fridge and kicked off her shoes. Sitting on the sofa in her living room, she tried again to imagine how her father would decide to hide his information. He had to find a way to fool Jack in case the book was found.

Touching the black ink in her father's familiar scrawl made her feel closer to him. She could imagine him sitting in his den at this time of the morning. Faye, Kristie and Sharyn were asleep. He knew their lives could be endangered by what he was doing. That's why he hid the book at the office. He hollowed out the spot behind the picture himself. Just the size he needed for the book. He looked up at the walls in his den. They were covered with fishing and racing memorabilia.

Fishing was a passion he shared with Jack. They'd spent long hours together with Caison on the lakes and rivers around the state. But racing was a hobby he didn't share with the other two men. Caison and Jack knew nothing about the drivers or their cars.

Sharyn jumped up when she realized what her father had done. He'd correlated the numbers of drivers and racing dates to the information he was gathering for the FBI. Once she understood, the pages came alive in her hands. She hurried to translate the entire code book then burned all the information on her computer to a CD just as the sun was peeking through the clouds across the mountains. With the disc in her hand, she erased what she'd put into the computer. Then she hid the code book back in the spot behind her medicine cabinet. First thing in the morning, she'd put the disc into her safety deposit box at the bank.

"Good work, Dad. I think we'll see Jack behind bars yet."

Chapter Seven

Sharyn was too excited to sleep. She spent the night going over her figures, making sure everything was right. The code made sense now. It was a schedule for things being delivered to Diamond Springs, Duke's Stag-Inn-Doe and various other parts of the county.

Her father tagged them according to what the shipment was; guns, drugs, bootleg videotapes, etc. He used the amalgams of his favorite drivers' names for places, their car numbers for what was being delivered, and their points and standing on the date of the shipment. It was brilliant.

There were no names. But she was sure the FBI agents would know who he was talking about. Her father's code book would fill in the rest. It struck her at about 4 A.M. that bringing Jack Winter down probably meant further destroying Caison Talbot.

Knowing her mother wasn't going to be happy about losing the ex-senator again, Sharyn paid an early morning call at their old house. She hadn't seen her in a few days, and somehow she hoped she could explain or prepare her for what was coming. She didn't think about Caison being there with her that early. Even worse, he looked like he'd spent the night.

Taking a big gulp of coffee and bacon-filled air, Sharyn fixed a smile on her face and sat down with them at the same table she'd shared with her family growing up.

"It's good to see you." Her mother smiled and blushed. "Sit down and eat something. You look like a rail!"

"You've always encouraged her to lose weight, Faye," Caison reminded her. "She looks great!"

"Never mind." Faye pulled out a chair for her daughter. "Juice?"

"Thanks." Sharyn sat down and had some juice and toast with them. Every time she tried to broach the subject she came to discuss, she found the words sticking in her mouth. It was too weird sitting there like that with Caison. He was one of her father's close friends but not her father. He was sitting in her father's chair, smiling at her mother. Faye brushed his cheek with her hand as she leaned close to pour his coffee. She'd used the same gesture with T. Raymond.

"I have something I want to show you," Faye said while Sharyn tried to swallow dry toast down her drier throat. "Wait until you see it! I went shopping yesterday."

When they were alone, Caison looked up from his paper. "I know this must be hard for you, Sharyn. And you know I'd never try to take your father's place."

"You couldn't." She drank her juice with deliberation. She was thirsty but the orange juice tasted like sour milk to her.

The ex-senator, famous for his hearty filibusters, shook his head. His shock of snow-white hair played up his keen blue eyes and tanned face. "You're going to have to live with it, young woman. I love your mother."

"Enough to give her up before she's embarrassed again?" She didn't mean to say it. The words slipped out before she could recall them.

"What are you talking about?"

"She was embarrassed when she found out you weren't really a widower and had a son you never claimed," she reminded him in a quiet voice with a glance at the empty hallway. "How's she going to feel when they take you to prison for killing my father because he knew what you and Jack and Duke were doing?"

Caison's ruddy features blanched. "What are you saying?"

Sharyn knew she'd said too much. She backed down, mumbling something unintelligible until she saw her mother come out of her bedroom. Loose lips, she chided herself. How many times had she warned her deputies? Here she was doing the same thing.

Faye made her grand entrance in an ivory colored suit and a veiled ivory hat. "What do you think?"

"You look great," Sharyn told her. "Have you set a date for the wedding?"

"We're thinking about November." Faye smiled at Caison. "I think we've waited long enough."

Sharyn cleared her throat and smiled, getting up to kiss her mother on the cheek. "That's great. Let me know what I can do to help."

"Keep out of trouble?" Faye suggested. "Don't get hurt or have to work that day. I'd like to have you at the wedding. If you can manage that, we'll be doing fine."

"I'll be there," Sharyn promised, glancing at Caison who still looked stunned. "But I have to go."

"I know." Faye patted her shoulder. "You're trying to get Ed out of trouble. That wasn't something I wanted to hear on the news. Everyone knows Ed didn't kill that man. It was probably one of Duke's drug contacts! It was smart for you to ask Caison to defend Ed."

Caison picked up his newspaper in a shaky hand and excused himself, hiding behind it.

"I'll talk to you later, Mom." Sharyn kissed her mother again, not sure how Faye was going to take any revelations about her fiancé coming from her. Faye knew she wasn't fond of Caison. She wasn't looking forward to it. But there was no escaping the truth. If Caison was involved, he would go to prison.

Sharyn called the pager number Agent Brewster gave her. He called her back immediately and arranged to meet her at the old Union Cemetery just outside of town. She got there first and had a chance to look around. The Historical Society had done a great job cleaning up. Even the excavation the sheriff's department did to remove the Mercedes they found buried there was barely visible.

Thinking back to that case brought her no pleasure, even though she solved the crime. Up until now, she only thought about her cases until they were over. It was in her nature to finish with something and put it behind her. But realizing she may have missed some important clues while she investigated the death of Trudy's husband made her question all of the arrests she'd made. Were they the right people? How many mistakes *had* she made?

Even in the case of her father's murder, she'd missed an important element. She arrested the two obvious men but didn't think about someone pulling their strings. At that time, she was oblivious to the darkness that claimed parts of her hometown.

She realized she couldn't go back and re-think every case she'd investigated. And she couldn't spend all of her time questioning herself or she wouldn't get anything done. But what was the alternative? Haphazardly finding killers and thieves then hoping she had the right people?

"Sheriff." Agents Brewster and Gallagher approached her from behind the cemetery. "We didn't expect to hear from you so quickly."

She glanced at the road. There was no sign of their car. They had to get there before her and walk in from the woods. "There was something I didn't tell you. Actually, I wasn't sure it was something worth mentioning until last night. I found a small book written in code. It was hidden in my father's old office. I recognize his handwriting in it."

Brewster nodded. "He told me he was keeping a record. I thought it was destroyed."

Gallagher actually smiled. "Good work, Sheriff! Did you bring it with you?"

She took the CD out of her pocket. "I deciphered it at home last night and burned a copy. I still have the original. It's in a safe place."

"We can make this work for us," Brewster promised.

"Everyone will know that your father died to protect this. That can make quite an impact on a jury."

"How's your investigation going?" Sharyn asked. "I believe our DA will talk to me today about filing charges against my deputy. His wife seems to be in the clear. But that makes it more important that your investigation moves forward."

Gallagher patted his pocket. "With this CD, we can move a lot faster, Sheriff. It's not like your deputy will go to trial tomorrow. He may even get bail. Who knows?"

"If he doesn't, he'll be transported to the county jail. He's been with the sheriff's department over twenty years. He's bound to have a lot of enemies out there. Even if he isn't put in with the general population, his life will be in danger."

"Don't worry," Brewster reassured her. "We'll either have this wrapped up in the next few days or we'll have your deputy transferred somewhere safe. Either way we'll take care of the problem. We appreciate you working with us."

Sharyn nodded. "Thanks. Keep me informed."

Brewster and Gallagher stood in the soft clay and waited until Sharyn backed out into the road. She watched them walk back toward the woods before she pulled out on the main road that led to Diamond Springs. The two FBI agents seemed concerned about being seen with her. She hoped they were as careful with Ed's life as they were with their own.

The drive to the courthouse gave her a few more minutes to think about who killed Duke. Cutting a hole in the office window was a careful, deliberate act. It couldn't be one of anger or revenge. Only a professional wouldn't simply stand outside and shoot at the car. He or she had to be supremely confident. Hitting the car the first time was important. Did that mean someone hired a hit man to take care of Duke? All of those other close calls Trudy mentioned weren't working. Maybe whoever wanted Duke out of the way wasn't willing to wait anymore.

Like the two men who killed her father, Sharyn was convinced the 'talent' was local. All she had to do was find the shooter *and* the person behind him. A thing she'd probably missed with both her father and Trudy's husband.

Ernie was waiting for her when she got to the office. "Mr. Percy wants to see you *now*. He actually walked down here looking for you."

That surprised her. Eldeon Percy never walked anywhere he didn't have to. "I suppose he wants to know why we're dragging our feet filing charges against Ed."

"I suppose." He glanced at her as he held open the door. "I was surprised you weren't here before me this morning getting everything set up for today. We have to find enough evidence to keep Ed out of jail."

"He has to make bail. We both know there's no other way right now. Caison agreed to represent him. That's in our favor. Ed was born and raised here and has been with the sheriff's department most of his life. That has to count for something. Everyone I know would put up their houses for collateral to get him out."

"What about the part that he's innocent so someone else did the crime?"

"That's true," she agreed. "But if Percy arraigns him today, we don't have time to prove it. Maybe we can still keep him out of the county jail using the legal system. It works sometimes."

Ernie's face mirrored his dislike of that plan. "I'd rather find the real killer. You know we're sitting on a time bomb, Sharyn. They don't have the weapon that killed Gunther *yet*. But it could happen today. Then everything will be messed up."

"One thing at a time," she advised as they approached the DA's office. She straightened her uniform and took off her hat. "Right now, let's get through this."

Mr. Percy's assistant met them at the door and offered them coffee. They both declined. "The DA is waiting to see you, Sheriff. Go right in."

"I hate this part," Ernie whispered to Sharyn. "I'd rather stand in a back alley with a gun stuck in my belly than be here."

"You've been here plenty of times. And no matter what, Mr. Percy's words aren't going to kill you."

"Good morning, Sheriff. Deputy. How nice of you to join me." Percy sat behind his desk, and the pale morning sunshine filtered through the blinds around him. Only the inflection of his voice gave away his impatience.

"Sorry Mr. Percy," Sharyn began. "We're in the middle of a homicide investigation. Sometimes that has to take priority."

Percy didn't move but his entire attitude shifted. "Don't lecture *me*, young woman. Even the sheriff is accountable for her time. That's why we give you various communication devices. None of these made you available to me this morning. Do you have something to hide?"

"Not at all. I was meeting with an informant. I thought my radio or cell phone going off might be a distraction. I'm sorry you couldn't reach me."

He nodded and motioned for them to sit down in the highback chairs set before his desk. "I want to talk to you about your deputy. I hope your lapse of communication wasn't due to your trying to get around this issue. Why weren't the appropriate papers filed after you arrested Deputy Robinson?"

Sharyn put her hat in her lap and folded her hands. "Deputy Robinson hasn't been charged with anything yet, sir."

He made a pyramid with his long, thin hands and sat back. "Now we come to the crux of the matter. Why *hasn't* he been charged, Sheriff?"

"Because we *know* he didn't do it." Her tone was matter of fact and her gaze never left his face.

"That's fine, Sheriff. Who *is* your suspect in this shooting?"

"We don't have one yet, sir. We're investigating."

Percy smiled and closed his eyes. "You found your deputy leaning over the rifle that shot Duke Beatty, a distinguished member of our community. Your deputy believed Mr. Beatty was involved in kidnapping his wife. He assaulted Mr. Beatty's employee for information. Your deputy then confessed to the crime in front of hundreds of people. What exactly are you investigating?"

"We both know Ed didn't kill Duke," Sharyn said. "I don't want to file charges against an innocent man."

"That's very noble of you. But as far as the people of Montgomery County are concerned, your deputy murdered Duke in a fit of anger and jealousy."

"Jealousy?" she asked. "Why would Ed be jealous of Duke?"

"Duke's employee, Mr. Martin, has given his statement. In it, he tells us that Ed's wife was flirting with Duke. She was spending a lot of time at the speedway and Duke's nightclub. I think that would make any man jealous, don't you, Deputy?" Percy switched his cold glance to Ernie.

Ernie shifted uncomfortably. "No way was Trudy interested in Duke. She was investigating him because she thought he killed her first husband. Ed didn't have anything to be jealous of."

"Oh? Deputy Robinson *knew* his wife was investigating Duke?"

"No, sir." The words sounded defeated, dragged from Ernie's lips.

"He only knew she was sneaking out to see him, isn't that right, Deputy?"

"Are we on trial here?" Ernie finally burst out. "We're investigating the evidence, Mr. Percy! Give us a few more days before you charge him."

The look on Percy's face spoke volumes on what he felt about being lectured and yelled at in his office. "I know you feel strongly about this, Deputy. But we all have jobs to do. I suggest you do yours. I intend to do mine. Deputy Robinson will be formally charged and arraigned at three P.M. this afternoon."

Ernie started to speak up again but Sharyn put her hand on his arm. "Thanks for the warning, Mr. Percy. We'll see you later. But for the record, Ed *didn't* kill Duke. And we'll prove it."

"I hope you do, Sheriff. A deputy who murders people isn't the sort of thing I want to see in Diamond Springs. I hope you feel the same."

"You can't win with that man," Ernie said when they were in the hall outside his office. "He has to know Ed isn't some rogue cop who went on a shooting spree. Why is he acting like this?"

"He's right," Sharyn replied. "It's his job. We're holding Ed for the shooting. Percy is following up. It's what he does."

"We only brought Ed in because he confessed and we had to," he argued. "Not because we think he did it."

"Let's get everyone together and see what other leads are out there."

"Yeah." Ernie wrestled with changing course in his thoughts. "I forgot to tell you. Nick called. He's got some stuff for us. Maybe something he has will help. 'Cause frankly, this isn't looking good for Ed. I'd like to shoot him myself for confessing like that. He knew better."

"He was protecting Trudy." Sharyn pushed open the door to the parking lot.

"Who probably won't be charged with either crime."

"Do you want her to be? Even to save Ed?"

"No, of course not." He took out his cell phone. "I'll let Cari know where we're going. Joe came in this morning. We got a call from one of the new sub-divisions. Someone was driving around in a van looking suspicious. I sent him out there."

"Did he go see Ed?"

"Yeah. Kicked his butt too." Ernie looked at Sharyn as he fastened his seatbelt. "Where were you this morning? Did you really meet with an informant? If so, when did we start doing things like that alone?"

Sharyn started the Jeep so she wouldn't have to look at him. She hated lying to him. "If you consider my mom and Caison as informants, then I guess they were clueing me in about their wedding in November."

"That sounds good. It's about time she forgave him."

"If it should *ever* be that time." Sharyn drove out of the parking lot. "I don't know, Ernie. Caison probably has a lot worse secrets. They might come out someday too."

"Sometimes a man can't come clean with everything," he told her. "I guess I know that first hand. All those years I kept that secret about the boy's school. I thought I was doing right, that telling people would hurt more than just me. Maybe Talbot feels the same. Maybe the things he isn't proud of would hurt a lot of people."

"Does that mean someone shouldn't be prosecuted for killing or stealing if it was a long time ago and bringing it out might hurt people?"

"No, I suppose not. All I'm saying is be sure your dislike of Talbot isn't just because he's trying to take your daddy's place. T. Raymond knew your mama couldn't live alone. He expected her to remarry when the time came. He always figured he'd go first."

Sharyn wanted to say more. She wanted to use the ammunition she had to convince him that Caison shouldn't marry her mother. But she couldn't. Instead, she pulled out on Main Street in the middle of the morning rush hour. She saw her ex-deputy get out of a black Ferrari in front of the police station. "Is David dating Julia Richmond again?"

Ernie whistled through his teeth as his head rotated to follow the shiny black sports car. "Maybe. That's Julia's car. I was wondering where he's been getting all those fancy toys of his lately. Charlie told me David showed him his new Rolex. He's definitely not living on a police officer's pay."

"I wonder if he's been to see Ed," Sharyn said.

"I don't know. There's been some bad blood between them since David quit us and moved next door. Ed says he quit going home much too. His sister is upset about it. David's an only child, you know."

Sharyn didn't know. She went to school with David but they weren't friends. He joined the sheriff's department while she was still in law school. It made their relationship difficult, even though David would've been last on the list to be the next sheriff.

They parked at the Diamond Springs hospital lot and went into the old basement. The morgue and crime scene lab were located there. The Historical Society wanted to do a full search of the basement to look for Confederate artifacts.

That part of the hospital had been in use since before the Civil War.

Nick told them they were welcome to do whatever they wanted *after* he retired. They appealed to the hospital board. The board sided with Nick and the matter was squashed. But anytime Sharyn was out with Nick and they passed a member of the Historical Society, she knew the older ladies would turn their heads and pretend not to see them.

"Well," Nick said when he saw her, "what brings you down here? Oh, that's right. I called you about a hundred times. Where were you?"

Sharyn hated lying to him almost as much as she hated lying to Ernie. But before she had to say anything. Ernie stepped in and did it for her.

"She was with her mother and Caison." Ernie took off his hat and made a face at Nick. "Do yourself a favor. Don't ask her about it. You don't want to hear all that whining. I know I didn't."

"Ernie!" Sharyn was glad he did such a good job covering for her but the whining part was a little overboard.

Nick laughed. "Hey, thanks for the warning. Since you're here, you might want to take a look at this."

"I hope you found something that proves Ed didn't shoot Duke." Ernie followed him. "If not, Mr. Percy will have him at the county jail tonight."

"I don't think I have anything that substantial," Nick said. "Sorry. But I did find a few interesting things." They went into the lab with him. "Take a look at this." He held up the small round part of the window from the racetrack office. "Can you see it?"

Ernie squinted at it. "What are we looking at?"

"A very fine strand of silk. Pink silk. Chinese, I think. The fibers are different because they drown the worms." Nick grinned at Sharyn. "I didn't know that until the sheriff told me. It snagged on the rough edge of the glass. Probably when it was cut."

"Does this mean whoever cut the hole out of the window

was wearing pink silk?" Ernie asked. "Because if so, we can take this to court this afternoon and free Ed. I dare *anyone* to find a pink silk blouse in Ed's closet."

"I wish it were that easy." Nick adjusted the microscope for them to see the fiber. "I couldn't swear it came from a blouse. It could've come from a tie or a robe. Hundreds of things are made from silk. If Trudy has pink silk blouse, a thread could've been transferred to Ed's shirt. This is too random to make any difference."

Sharyn looked at the thread on the lens. "Is there some way to track it down? Find out where it came from?"

"I don't know. If you find me a pink silk blouse, I can tell you if it was part of it. Otherwise, it might be useless."

"I was afraid you were going to say that." She moved away from the microscope. "Anything else?"

"Maybe." Nick picked up his black-rimmed glasses. "It's more an omission. Megan and Keith couldn't find the glass cutter. That probably means the killer took it with him."

"Great! So all we have to find is a killer wearing a pink blouse or tie who's carrying a glass cutter," Ernie lamented. "That's not so bad."

Nick shrugged. "Wish I had more for you but whoever killed Duke and Gunther was very careful to only leave evidence behind that convicted Trudy. The office was covered with her prints. If Ed wouldn't have confessed, you'd have her for both murders."

"I can't say that's a good thing," Ernie said. "Either way is just plain bad."

"Have you checked out the idea that the person who did this hated Trudy?" Nick asked. "You've been looking at the dead men but maybe they were superfluous. Maybe it could've been anyone who was killed."

Sharyn kissed Nick's cheek. "You stay here and look for more forensic evidence. Let us come up with conclusions."

"What? That wasn't so bad. Just because the hit looks professional doesn't mean anything," Nick argued. "Maybe the person who hates Trudy is a professional hit man.

Maybe the fact that Gunther was Duke's mechanic doesn't mean anything."

Ernie shook his head. "We want to prove Ed is innocent, old son, not send him away for life. Call us if you have any more *real* evidence."

"You mean like something from the Stag-Inn-Doe?" Nick called after them. "When I find out whose idea that was, I'm going to be wreaking some revenge. Do you know how filthy that place is? They should've burned it down after it started the black plague. Even if there *was* any evidence of a crime out there, it would be over the top of ten other crimes. What was someone thinking?"

"He really goes on, doesn't he?" Ernie said to Sharyn as they left the morgue with Nick still yelling at them.

"Talk about *me* whining!"

"So now what? Where do we go from here?"

"I'm not sure." Where did she dare go to try to prove Ed was innocent without giving anything away that would hurt the FBI investigation? On the other hand, what should she do to make it look real?

"Maybe we're after a female shooter," Ernie said. "I saw Nick's report this morning. The red mark on the rifle stock might be lipstick and we have a pink silk fiber from the glass. Maybe it was one of Duke's old girlfriends. It wouldn't necessarily make any sense about Gunther being killed too, but I'm not worried about that right now."

Sharyn shrugged. "It makes as much sense as anything else. I suppose we could talk to Marti about Duke's lady friends. Maybe there was one who was an expert marksman and wore silk blouses."

"I was thinking we could look at Ben's file too," he suggested. "If we missed something there, it might be good to know it. It might even help us find Duke's killer."

"Maybe," she admitted, not seeing how it could hurt to look back through it. "Although I think Duke was only mentioned as the owner of the car Ben died in."

"I know it's a long shot. But I can't think of anything

right now except Ed going to prison. My brain is only on autopilot."

"I know what you mean. Let's start with Marti and get out Ben's file. We've found things that brought convictions in places that made less sense."

When they got back to the courthouse, Roy was holding a press conference on the stairs of the pink granite building. Sharyn and Ernie waited to hear what he had to say before they went back to their office.

". . . I don't like it anymore than you all," Roy was saying, "but I don't have any evidence to prove that Ms. Robinson committed this crime. I have to release her. I have no choice but to proceed with my investigation from this point."

Foster Odom, the *Diamond Springs Gazette* reporter, pushed his way to the front. As usual he was wearing a black Panthers' cap and jacket. His greasy blond hair poked out from under the cap. "What about the gun?"

"We haven't located the weapon that killed Mr. Mabry," Roy told him. "If anyone finds a gun near the First Street pier, they should call or bring it by the police department."

"Is there a reward for the gun?" Odom asked.

"Not at this time."

"What about Duke?" someone shouted from the crowd. "What are you doing about the man who killed him?"

Roy's chest puffed out. "I'm afraid that's out of my hands. You'll have to take that up with Sheriff Howard."

More questions about Duke were shouted out but Roy ended the press conference, thanking them for coming. He passed Sharyn and Ernie on his way back into the court-house. "I hope you've got some answers for them, Sheriff. It's a mighty angry crowd out there. Duke was a hero. A man of the people. He'll be missed."

"He was a drug dealer, a womanizer and we don't know what all went on behind those sunglasses," Ernie shocked Sharyn by telling him. "But I'm sure they'd be glad to let you do his eulogy, Roy."

"I'm just glad the cases worked out this way, Deputy." Roy laughed. "I truly am."

"Let's go," Sharyn urged Ernie, amazed that he didn't defend his hero. "Standing here arguing with Roy isn't going to help Ed."

But when they went to talk to Marti Martin again, he was gone. The guard said that he'd been released by the DA after giving his statement.

"That's one boy we won't be seeing for a while." Ernie slammed his fist down on the desk. "I can't believe Mr. Percy didn't ask us before he let him go."

"At least there's still Ben's file to look through." Sharyn wondered if Percy's release had anything to do with the FBI trying to hold back the investigation. If so, did that mean the DA knew about the FBI? Somehow she'd always imagined him playing on the other team.

"What about the money Spunky Tucker owed Duke?" Trudy came up on them. "Has anyone checked into that idea?"

Sharyn hugged her. "How do you feel? Shouldn't you be home resting?"

"I'm fine." Trudy returned her embrace. "And resting is something I shouldn't be doing right now. Especially with my husband in jail for a crime he didn't commit."

Ernie gave Sharyn an I-told-you-so look and put his arm around Trudy's shoulders. "You know you can count on us to take care of this, honey. You should go home and get better. We'll take care of Ed."

Trudy extricated herself from his grasp and frowned at him. "Don't patronize me, Ernie Watkins! Now are you gonna come along or do I have to do this all myself?"

Chapter Eight

"Besides the obvious alibi that Spunky was standing next to me when Duke was killed," Sharyn drawled, "what makes you think he was involved in the shooting?"

"I heard them arguing one night when I was with Gunther," Trudy said. "He told me Spunky owed Duke twelve hundred dollars! Duke might've demanded it back. Spunky probably decided to kill him rather than pay. If you bring him in and squeeze him, he'll probably confess."

Ernie frowned and shook his head. "Squeeze him?"

"That's what they call it on TV. What's wrong?" Trudy asked, watching him. "That's a better motive than Ed had."

"True," Ernie agreed. "And if Ed hadn't confessed to the media, he probably wouldn't be locked up right now!"

"Spunky would've had to hire someone to kill Duke," Sharyn added. "It would've cost him more than he owed. It doesn't make any sense."

"What about one of Duke's lady friends?" Trudy suggested. "I know a few of them."

Sharyn glanced at Ernie. "We might be looking for a female shooter."

He shrugged and pulled at his hat. "It might be worth a try."

But four hours later, all they had to show for spending the time on the road was a string of young women with beauty

108

queen titles who all had alibis. Some of them were still in high school.

"Where are you going now?" Trudy asked as Sharyn backed the Jeep out of the last girl's driveway. Her parents didn't know that she was dating the famous race car driver. They weren't pleased, even though the girl denied it. Trudy told them she'd seen the girl at the Stag and the father almost exploded.

"Back to the office," Sharyn answered. "We were about to look up Ben's records when you found us. I think that's what we need to do now."

"All right." There was a resolute purpose to Trudy's face. "I'll see what's happening out at the track. There's bound to be someone there."

"That's not a good idea," Ernie said. "You're only making this worse for yourself."

Sharyn agreed. "Go home, Trudy. You've been through a lot. Get some rest. This isn't over for *you* yet either. We'll let you know if we find anything. I'm going to get you in to see Ed before his arraignment this afternoon."

"I appreciate your help. But I can't sit at home and let Ed take the fall for what happened. I'm guiltier than he is. It's not fair for him to be in there."

Ernie reminded her, "Don't worry. If your gun turns up and it's a match for the bullet Nick took out of Gunther, you'll be right in there keeping Ed company."

"All right! You've made your point!" Trudy got out when Sharyn parked in the impound lot. She slammed the door. "I'll go home. I'd appreciate it, Sharyn, if I could see Ed."

"Do you need a ride home?" Sharyn asked her, feeling a pang of remorse after her hard words.

"No. My car is out front. I'll be fine."

"I'll call you," Sharyn promised.

They watched Trudy walk toward the street. "Do you think she paid any attention to us at all?" Ernie asked.

"I doubt it." Sharyn sighed. "I just hope she doesn't do something stupid."

"You mean like Ed?" Ernie whistled between his teeth. "I never realized how perfectly matched the two of them are!"

They went back to the office and pulled the files on Ben's death. It was strange reading back over the notes, viewing the photos they'd taken two years ago. The investigation seemed to make sense. Gunther's alibi checked out. All of the pit crew was accounted for. Duke was at the Stag that night, drinking with some friends, one of them the mayor of Diamond Springs.

"Of course, anyone could've lied about Gunther or Duke," Ernie said. "And seeing the crowd they ran with, somebody probably covered for them."

"Possibly. If we understood what really happened that night, we might be able to pinpoint a suspect. But was Gunther trying to kill Duke or was Duke trying to kill Ben?"

"It never made sense to me that Gunther wasn't there that night. He was Duke's head mechanic. Shouldn't he have been working on the car?"

Sharyn picked up the copy of Gunther's statement. "Apparently, he was only there if Duke was racing. He found out Duke wasn't racing and went home. Three witnesses there saw him leave the track before the race. There are two other mechanics who work for the team. It wasn't unusual for Gunther not to be there at the smaller races."

Ernie nodded as he looked through another part of the file. "It seems like we talked to everyone. But if Trudy's right, we missed something."

"I don't see any way Gunther could've been responsible for Ben's death." Sharyn put down the papers she held. "The car was checked out before Ben drove it. Gunther didn't come near it again. Then Ben was killed in it. Unless all of them were lying to cover up for Gunther, it had to be someone else."

Ernie looked at her over the top of the file folder. "Let's say Gunther *did* set up the car for Duke to be killed, like Trudy said, and Duke was cagey enough not to drive it. It seems like he would've found some way to get rid of Gunther. We should've found Gunther's dead body two years ago."

"Instead, Duke kept him on. He must've felt safe with him."

"So maybe Gunther *didn't* try to kill Duke. Maybe Trudy got it messed up. But if that's the case, why was Gunther killed?"

"Maybe it was an accident. Maybe Trudy can't remember shooting him. Maybe he drugged her and took her out in the boat. She was conscious enough to remember she had the gun with her." Sharyn leaned heavily on her desk. "Maybe Trudy killed Gunther. It would've been self-defense."

Ernie thought about it and didn't like it. "Maybe. But it seems too coincidental Duke was killed too. Not to mention that Trudy was in both places. If they'd left it with her killing Gunther, I might've bought it. With her being at the track too, it smells too much like a setup to me. We saw what kind of shape she was in. How did she get from the lake to the speedway?"

"You know I like your idea better. I don't want to think Trudy shot Gunther for any reason." Sharyn glanced at her watch. "We need to meet her upstairs if she's going to see Ed before the arraignment."

One of the volunteers brought Sharyn a call from the highway patrol. A climber was stranded on the side of Diamond Mountain. He was hanging on a rope, dangling over the Interstate.

"Thanks." Sharyn took it from him. "People need to think a little before they try the face. First-time climbers always end up like this."

"I'll take it," Ernie said. "I can't do anything to help Ed in that courtroom. I'd rather be out working than thinking about it."

"Okay." Sharyn was surprised but didn't remark on it. "I'll let you know how it turns out."

Ernie's brown eyes leveled with hers. "It will take a miracle to get him out on bail. Maybe Caison can pull it off. We'll see."

Sharyn met Caison in the courthouse lobby. He still looked formidable in his proper dark suit and white shirt. He reminded her of pictures she'd seen of Andrew Jackson. His harsh features had softened a little in the last few years. But determination and intelligence were marked in his stern face.

"I was wondering if you were going to show." He grabbed her hand in a strong handshake.

"Why wouldn't I? You're doing me a favor taking Ed's case." Sharyn tried to keep her personal feelings about him away from the case. She needed him to be there for Ed. She didn't have to like him. At least she knew he wasn't associated with the good old boys' network anymore. Jack had stolen everything from him. She knew he wasn't the forgiving type.

"After your visit this morning, I wasn't so sure. Apparently, even *you* can be corrupted."

"I guess I don't see it so much as corruption," she explained. "It took Mothra to beat Godzilla."

He looked puzzled but laughed at her comparison. "I guess you're right about that. But aren't you afraid this will come up when you turn over your evidence to the FBI and have me arrested?"

"I can honestly say I don't know for sure yet that you were involved in what happened to my father. I *know* Jack was. I'm sure there were a few others. I'm guessing the two of you aren't such good friends anymore since he took your senate seat." She studied his face. "You could come forward and turn state's evidence against him."

"I could also climb up on my roof and jump off," he quipped. "You better be thinking about that too, young woman. He likes you now. You're a shiny new toy. But if you push him too hard, you might wish you'd jumped off *your* roof. Take it from me. Jack makes a bad enemy."

Sharyn took a step closer to him. "Just tell me one thing. Were you involved in having my father killed? Or was that all Jack's idea?"

Caison pulled his tall, thin frame upright. "I don't know what you're talking about, Sheriff. But an accusation like that can get you into serious trouble. A less respectable man might take that as a lead-in to a lawsuit."

"Hey there!" Trudy called out to them and ran across the lobby. "I hope there's still time to see Ed before the trial." She shook Caison's hand. "I really appreciate you defending my husband. You know, I always voted for you."

"Thank you, Trudy. And you're welcome. We better get going." Caison nodded towards the stairs. "Let's see what Deputy Robinson has to say for himself."

The guard brought Ed to a small meeting room. Sharyn dismissed the guard and closed the door behind them. Ed and Trudy kissed and held each other without speaking. Caison and Sharyn studied the old tile floor as the couple embraced.

After a long moment, Caison said, "Thank you for your help, Sheriff. You'll have to wait outside now."

Sharyn stared at him, not understanding. "I'm Ed's friend. There's nothing he can tell you that will make any difference to me."

"You're also the sheriff of this county," he reminded her. "Anything you hear you could be compelled to use against my client. I know you're close to him. But this is different. You know that. You understand more about the law than most. I shouldn't have to tell you."

She knew he was right. Technically, she was prosecuting Ed for the county. She might not be the DA but she was his right hand. She couldn't help Ed any further even though she wanted to be there for him as his friend.

"You can stay," Ed told her, his arm around Trudy. "I don't have anything to hide. I don't care about the legal stuff."

"Then you better start caring," Sharyn told him. "As much as I hate it, Mr. Talbot's right. I'm the sheriff and you're my prisoner. That's the way it is right now."

"Let me decide about the legal matters, Deputy. That's what I'm here for." Caison opened his briefcase. "Go on now,

Sharyn. We have work to do and precious little time to do it."

Sharyn smiled at Ed. "It's okay. I'll wait outside." She walked out of the room and closed the door behind her. It was terrible not being able to do anything. The FBI had her hands tied as sheriff while it worked its investigation. Being sheriff kept her from being personally involved with Ed on this. It was like being trapped by her identity.

Ernie probably realized it would be this way. That's why he decided to go out on the call. She had years of legal education as well as the experience of being sheriff, but she was blinded by her emotions in this case. Ernie still had better instinct than she did sometimes. She knew he was right about Ed being in serious trouble. Unless someone came up with another viable suspect, a trial would go against him.

Fifteen minutes later, the court bailiff and the security guard came for Ed. Caison went with him to the courtroom. Trudy grabbed Sharyn's hand as they walked behind them. "I'm scared to death for him," she admitted with tears in her eyes. "I wish he'd been quiet and let them try to prosecute me for this."

It was strange trying to reassure Trudy. She was more like her aunt than her assistant. How many times had Trudy been there for her? Sharyn squeezed her hand and smiled at her, tried to comfort her but she was worried too. Going into the county jail population was one thing. The possibility of going to prison was an even grimmer specter. Ed had worked as a deputy for most of his adult life. The chances weren't good that he'd make it through even a short time in prison.

They found seats behind Ed. Judge White was presiding. Trudy glanced at Sharyn as they sat down in the crowded courtroom. "No-bail White," she whispered. "The only one who might have been worse is Judge Daily. He takes those long fishing trips with Mr. Percy. I think they're related by marriage too. One of their cousins or some such. Couldn't we ask for a mistrial or something?"

"Not yet," Sharyn said. It wasn't a good sign. Usually, she liked Judge White. He was strictly according to the book, but kept the bad guys in jail. In this case, the bad guy was her friend. A strict interpretation of the law wasn't such a good thing. She couldn't believe everything was so messed up.

Joe sat down beside her. "I thought you'd be here." He clapped Ed on the shoulder and nodded to his friend.

Sharyn looked at Joe. "Who's minding the store?"

"Ernie's back. Cari's there. I'm staying for the hearing. There has to be something we can do to keep him out of county." He took off his hat and sunglasses. His spiky dark hair emphasized his strong cheekbones and pointed chin.

"All rise," the bailiff called out as the courtroom became still. "The honorable Judge Harrison White presiding for the criminal court of Montgomery County, North Carolina."

Sharyn looked back at the entryway. Eldeon Percy was sashaying to the prosecutor's table. Beside him was Senator Jack Winter. A buzz went through the courtroom. It was unusual enough to see the DA at an arraignment. For a state senator to accompany him was noteworthy. Both men sat down at the front table. Jack smiled at Caison and offered him his hand.

The two men stared at each other. A moment later, Caison gathered his papers and briefcase and started to leave the room. The spectator buzz turned to open discussion. Ed got to his feet. A security guard pressed him back down into his seat.

Judge White demanded to know what was going on. "Your client is already here, Mr. Talbot. It's too late to go out for a drink of water, sir."

Caison turned back to him. "I'm afraid I'm unable to defend this man, Your Honor. My health is precarious and I'm experiencing difficulties that may be another heart attack."

"Bailiff, call nine-one-one!" Judge White roared. "And find me a public defender!"

Sharyn, Trudy and Joe rushed to Caison's side. He sat down on a bench in the hall while his aid went to get him a glass of water. "I'm sorry, Sharyn. I can't do this. I hope you understand."

"Don't worry about it," she said. "EMS will be here soon. You'll be fine."

He grasped her hand tightly, forcing her to look into his face. "I'm not *sick!* I wish I were. I had to say something or my legal career would be over too! I can't go through with the trial. I can't get on their radar again. Do you understand? Not after last time. I have another chance now, if I keep my head low. Jack won't let me do this. I'm sorry."

She understood. She wished she didn't. "I'll find someone else." She took her hand from him. "Ed should get some kind of postponement, shouldn't he?"

"Probably. Maybe. *If* he had someone to argue for him."

"I'll find someone." Sharyn started back into the courtroom. She didn't have to look any further. Trudy was already standing beside Ed at the defense table.

"Your Honor, my husband has lost his attorney. He needs time to confer with a new one."

Sharyn saw the almost imperceptible nod that passed from Mr. Percy to Judge White. "This is only an arraignment. How does Deputy Robinson plead?"

Trudy looked baffled and Ed shrugged. "Not guilty," he said. "I didn't kill anyone. I said I did to keep Trudy out of jail. But—"

"That will do, Deputy! This isn't the trial. You'll have your opportunity to speak and be heard." Judge White banged his gavel on the desk. "Due to the serious nature of this crime and for the protection of the general public, Edward Robinson is held over for trial. No bail."

Sharyn stepped forward. "Your honor, Deputy Robinson was born and raised in this county. He has strong ties to the community besides being a dedicated public servant for over twenty years. You must be aware of the life-threatening situation county jail will put him in."

"Sheriff Howard? Are you representing the defendant instead of prosecuting him?" Judge White looked puzzled.

"No, sir," she said, feeling like that hiker hanging above

the Interstate on a thin line. "I'm just trying to see that justice is served until Deputy Robinson has a chance to consult with another attorney."

He seemed to consider the matter then ruled against her. "Your concern is duly noted, Sheriff. But when a public servant turns against the public he defends, drastic measures need to be taken. My ruling stands."

Trudy sagged, sitting down in the chair as Judge White left the courtroom. Ed put his arms around her and the security guard looked the other way for a few minutes. He'd played poker with Ed on lots of long winter nights.

EMS came for Caison. He let them take his blood pressure and look in his eyes. Then he pushed them aside and strode out of the courthouse. Sharyn found Joe sitting on the bench where she'd left the ex-senator.

"Well, that was something." He drank the glass of water Caison left. "What do you think happened?"

"I think he was terrified," Sharyn replied. "He lost almost everything last time he got in Jack's way. He's lucky to be alive. I didn't think the big guns would come in. I guess Caison didn't either."

People were streaming out of the courtroom, talking loudly about what happened. A reporter from the local television station was setting up with her cameraman to do a live feed. "In a surprise move, Judge Harrison White decreed that Deputy Ed Robinson would be held without bond awaiting trial on his first-degree murder charge in the shooting death of race car driver, Duke Beatty."

Joe put on his sunglasses. "I'm going to find out when they'll be picking Ed up. I'll see you back at the office."

"Okay." Sharyn wished she could say something else. She hadn't felt so powerless since she was a child. There was nothing she could do to keep Ed from going to the county facility. She couldn't believe Judge White preempted Ed's legal right to counsel. It would be a good reason for an appeal—if Ed survived to ask for one.

"Sharyn!" Jack's voice reached her through the crowd as he came up close to her. "I was hoping to talk with you."

She stared into his cold eyes, noticing how much his new found power suited him. He was looking fit and healthy, his complexion tanned and firm. "Senator," she acknowledged, then walked toward the stairs.

"This is such a disappointment," he said, following her through the door to the stairwell. "I know you weren't expecting your deputy to be held for trial. I know *I* wasn't. Especially in these circumstances."

"Whatever." She glanced back at him as she continued to move quickly down the stairs toward the ground floor. "Like you didn't know Caison would fold like wet tissue paper when he saw you. You want Ed to take the fall for this to cover your part in this."

"That's some plain speaking." He put his hand on her arm to stop her. "Let me be just as blunt. Your deputy made himself the sacrificial lamb in all of this. You can't blame me for his confession."

She shrugged off his hand. "Get away from me, Jack!"

"Sharyn, I've never made a secret of my admiration for you. If you want this to go another way, all you have to do is say the word."

"What would that word be?" she demanded, stopping again to stare at him.

He smiled and caressed her cheek. "Give up this dead-end job. Come to work for me in Raleigh on my staff. Let's get to know each other. There's an attraction. I know you feel it too."

"And you'd take care of this problem with Ed for me?"

"You know I would."

She smiled back at him. "Where is a tape recorder when you need one?"

"Sharyn—"

"The only thing I'm going to do is bring you down, Jack," she promised. "You've screwed up here or you wouldn't be working so hard to cover it up, would you? Imagine having to make a personal appearance! You must be losing your touch."

His smile didn't waiver from his thin lips. "I think your temper must be what I love best about you. You plunge head-first into everything. I imagine Nick appreciates your . . . drive as well?"

"Enjoy your life while you can." She started down the stairs again. "Prison orange won't look good on you."

He didn't follow her this time. She skipped down the stairs and out into the watery sunshine, taking a deep breath of the clean air. She knew she was right about him being there in court that day. Years ago, he wouldn't have needed to be there to make sure his will was done. Now she knew he was involved in Duke's death. But how? What was the connection between them?

She thought about blowing the whole FBI investigation to keep Ed out of jail. Only believing in the system and making herself remember that the investigation could prove who was behind her father's death made her stay quiet. A few more days, she reminded herself. Maybe they could find some way to hold up his transfer. It meant finally getting Jack and proving to everyone that her father was clean. Surely she could find some way to make it happen.

She walked back to the sheriff's office and started going through the photos and information they'd gathered so far on the case. Ernie was at his desk going through Duke's personal papers they'd taken from his home and office. Cari and Joe were out on patrol, leaving the phones and minor details to volunteers.

"It looks like Duke got a healthy deposit every month from someplace called RR Enterprises." Ernie brought her a copy of the bank statement. "Went in every month like clockwork. Only last month, it got to be a mite more."

Sharyn's brows rose at the jump in income. "Wow! I wish I got a raise that size." She glanced up at him. "Maybe he got greedy, huh? Let's find out who RR Enterprises is."

"That's what I was thinking." He looked at the file on her desk. "Find anything?"

"Not really. Right offhand, I'd say someone got fed up

with him and took him out. But whoever it was had to be local or he or she wouldn't care what it looked like. They wouldn't have needed Trudy for a scapegoat."

"Good point."

Her cell phone rang. It was Trudy. The DA was offering Ed a deal. Mr. Percy would let him plead to a lesser crime, manslaughter. "He's telling Ed the state already has him on Duke's murder through his own confession. He's offering to let Ed take the blame for Gunther's killing too and waive trial by saying he was so worried about me that he didn't know what he was doing."

"Is Ed going to take it?" Sharyn asked. She should've known they wouldn't wait to see what came out in a trial. If they could get Ed to plead to manslaughter, everything would be wrapped up nice and tidy.

"He doesn't know what to do. I don't know what to tell him. If he faces a first-degree murder charge, he could get the death penalty. If he takes the deal, his life is over. My life is over too. I don't know what to do."

"I'll be right there," Sharyn told her. "Don't let him do or say anything until we get him a new lawyer."

"They told him the deal was only for today. If he leaves the DA's office, the deal is off."

"Never mind, Trudy. Don't let him take that deal! I know it looks bad right now but what they're offering is worse!"

"I'll tell him what you said."

"I have to go," Sharyn told Ernie as she hung up the phone. "The DA is offering Ed a deal on both murders."

"What?" Ernie couldn't believe it. "They can't do that, can they? Ed won't take it will he?"

"I don't know. I'm going to check it out. See what you can find out about the deposit!"

Sharyn ran back into the courthouse. It was starting to rain again. The smooth stone steps on the courthouse were slippery with it. A gray haze surrounded the top of Diamond Mountain when she looked up at it. It was going to be foggy that night. Lots of wrecks on the roads. People didn't seem to understand that they needed to slow down when fog wrapped the area.

She remembered the old axiom Aunt Selma had taught her about fog in September. The number of fogs equaled the number of snowstorms in the winter. So far, they'd had six. If folklore held true, and it often did in the ancient hills, they'd be in for a heavy winter.

Workers were leaving the courthouse as she walked through the rotunda. She looked up at the painting on the ceiling. It depicted the first settlement around the lake that came to be known as Palmer. After WWII when the wealthy socialites stopped coming there to drink the water and breathe the healthy air, the name changed to Diamond Springs. It showed the bright sun shining on the lake and the happy faces of the people living good lives.

She remembered going there as a child to visit the courthouse. Kids teased her about her father being the sheriff. But she was always proud of her family's heritage. She looked up at that scene and believed they were part of keeping the town safe for all those smiling people. Years later, she still felt the same. There might be a bad element in Diamond Springs but mostly it was a great place to live. It was her job to get rid of the bad element.

But right now, she had to save Ed from himself. She met Trudy upstairs outside the DA's office. "Is he in there?"

Trudy nodded, her hands knit tightly together. "They didn't want me in there anymore. I guess you can't go in either. Like Caison said, technically you're on their side. You can't be the sheriff and help Ed."

"There has to be something we can do."

"There may not be something *you* can do, Sheriff," a husky male voice told her, "but I'd like to offer my services."

Sharyn couldn't believe George Albert was there. He looked older, sadder but up to the challenge in a sharp black suit and striped tie. "George!" She hugged him. "When did you get back?"

"I've been back for a while. I've just been keeping a low

profile. I wasn't ready to see everyone again. Brenda is still hiding out." He squared his shoulders and adjusted his tie. "But when I heard about Caison bailing on Ed, I knew it was time for me to come out of the shadows. I've lived with my shame and guilt for a long time. I think there might be a few good years left yet. I'd like to start them by helping Ed."

Trudy hugged him too. "You don't have anything to feel bad about, George. You loved Richard and you couldn't help the way he was. You did the best you could."

"I don't know about that," he disagreed. "But I appreciate the sentiment. Now let's talk about Ed. What's going on in there?"

Trudy explained about the DA's deal. "He didn't do it, George. You know Ed. He didn't kill Duke Beatty or Gunther Mabry. But if he thinks it will save me, he might say he did."

George picked up his briefcase and smiled at her. "Don't worry about a thing. Caison might be scared of those termites but I'm not. I'll take care of Ed."

Chapter Nine

Sharyn couldn't believe George was back or how good it was to see his face again. It was like finding an old friend still alive after she thought he was dead. He'd left Diamond Springs and his county commission seat three years ago after shooting his son, Richard, to save her life. It was a tragic story and the aftermath drove George and his wife away from the area.

George was one of her father's good friends. He comforted her, Faye and Kristie when T. Raymond was killed. He encouraged Sharyn to take her father's place as sheriff and became her sounding board when the other members of the sheriff's department had a hard time accepting her. He was her shoulder to cry on and a strong voice of reason in her young, inexperienced mind. If anyone could help resolve the problem Ed created for himself, it was George Albert.

Sharyn waited with Trudy on the hard wood bench outside the DA's office while the janitorial staff began cleaning up after the day's activities. It seemed like forever, made worse by not knowing what was going on inside. But finally, Ed was escorted out by a guard.

He stopped and kissed Trudy. "Don't cry, honey. It's gonna be okay. I didn't take the deal. George thinks we can beat this." He gave Sharyn a meaningful look. "Even if we *can't* find the real killer because the sheriff is too busy being my cheerleader. What are you doing out here?"

"What do you think?" Sharyn hugged him. "In the eyes of the law, we might have to stay separate, but you're family to me. I can't separate myself from that. We'll find the killer. Don't worry. Ernie is working a new angle now."

"That's what I want to hear." His face looked a little gaunt and he needed a shave but his blue eyes were filled with hope. "I can't believe George came back."

"I know!" Sharyn squeezed his arm. "I'll talk to you later."

Trudy walked back with him to the holding cell. Sharyn waited for George and Percy. They came out a few minutes later. Percy invited George and his wife, Brenda, to his house for a cookout when the weather cleared. George accepted and Percy nodded to Sharyn.

Sharyn wanted to hold her tongue but the words came tumbling out. "I can't believe you tried to force Ed to take a plea for murders you *know* he didn't commit. Was Jack pushing you that hard, Mr. Percy?"

Percy's eyes hardened. "I suggest you take care what you're saying, Sheriff. Judge White and I are in the arena of justice. I believe you're supposed to be part of that process whether your friend is involved or not."

She would've said more but George drew her away, telling her she wasn't helping Ed that way. Sharyn nodded to Mr. Percy reluctantly and walked away with her old friend. She didn't want to leave it that way but there was too much at stake to foul things up now. She had to be patient, for once.

"You didn't have to wait for me," George said to her when they were alone. "But I'm glad you did. Come home with me for dinner. I know Brenda would love to see you."

"Thanks. I'd love to see her too."

"We were so proud of you when we heard you won the election." They walked together towards the back parking lot. "Things have changed around here some. But some things never change."

"I've thought about you and Brenda so many times. I always hoped you didn't hate me for what happened."

He put his arm around her shoulders. "You're like a daughter to us. Always have been. Always will be. What happened with Richard was inevitable. I can see that now. I wish every day I'd seen it sooner. While we were gone, Brenda and I hoped you didn't hate *us* for what happened."

"You know I feel the same way I always have about the two of you. Where are you staying? I know you sold your house while you were gone."

He shrugged. "Too many bad memories. We bought a new place in one of the subdivisions right outside of town. Diamond Acres. You know it?"

"I do. It's a nice place. I'll follow you out there. I hope you don't mind me wearing the uniform at dinner."

"Not at all." He smiled at her. "You look good, Sharyn. Strong. Happy. You remind me so much of your father. I hear you're a good sheriff. I'll give Brenda a call on the cell phone to let her know we're coming."

It was strange being in the new house, eating dinner alone with Brenda and George. While George had been like a mentor for her in those first dark days after her father's death, the couple was her parents' friends. She and Kristie came with them for cookouts and Christmas parties. They played with Richard and went for canoe rides in the lake.

Being there alone pointed up how much times had changed. Brenda was excited and happy to see her. Sharyn barely recognized her. She'd lost so much weight and the shadows under her eyes told their own story of grief and loss. The dinner was nice but Sharyn couldn't help but feel she'd be more comfortable with her mother or Aunt Selma there with her. It was a small thing, a remnant of childhood. She pushed it aside and tried to enjoy her time with them.

While Brenda made coffee and fetched some homemade pound cake, Sharyn talked to George about Ed's case. "I appreciate you taking this on. I'll bet Mr. Percy was surprised to see you."

"You know I shouldn't be talking to you about this." He

folded his hands in his lap and nodded at her. "That uniform belongs behind the prosecutor, not the defendant."

"Ed's not guilty of anything except stupidity and loving Trudy. I know you're right about my place in all this. I'm just glad to know someone I can trust is looking after him."

"I'll do the best I can. I know Ed didn't kill Duke. The question is, who did? Old Duke probably had it coming for the last twenty years or so. I don't know who finally got enough courage to kill him, but I tip my hat to the man or woman. The man was a swine, hiding behind his façade of respectability."

Sharyn smiled. "Ernie is mourning him. There wasn't anybody like Duke as far as he was concerned."

"I'm sure there'll be a thousand others! I remember the first time I went out to the Stag-Inn-Doe," he reminisced. "I was sixteen but my ID said I was eighteen. That was before Duke's time. It was even wilder out there then. Barker Rosemont owned the place. He was famous for fighting the revenuers. He had the biggest still in the county. No one ever found it either, at least not until he was ready for them. That still is in a museum now. That's what I mean about times changing. If you live long enough, you see it all."

"Barker Rosemont," Sharyn repeated. "I know that name. I'm sure it wasn't in a history book."

"He married Maggie Childers. Her family still lives in Bells Creek. They're well connected in the area. A lot of people say that Duke murdered Barker for the Stag. It happened during a poker game. Everyone testified that it was self-defense, that Barker drew his gun first and accused Duke of cheating. Duke ran 'shine for Barker when he was a kid. He probably knew the boy pretty well."

"Here's the cake." Brenda re-entered the room with a flourish. "Chocolate double-butter, triple-egg, cream pound cake. I hope you're not on a diet, Sharyn. This would make one of those skinny runway models balloon up."

Sharyn had the coffee and only a small taste of pound cake. "I don't dare have any more after that warning." The cake was good but she knew she'd pay for it later if she had more.

They sat and talked for another twenty minutes or so until

they ran out of things to say and the hour edged toward ten.

"Don't be a stranger," Brenda told her when she was getting ready to leave.

Sharyn hugged her and promised to come back. "Mom will want to see you. She's marrying Caison Talbot in November. I know she'll want you to come."

The silence that followed her announcement was poignant. She looked into the shocked, unhappy faces of her mother's friends and felt the need to add, "He's changed a lot since he had his heart attack and lost his senate seat to Jack." It was hard for her to believe she was defending Caison.

George recovered first. "I'm sure he has. Everyone deserves another chance." He put his arm around Brenda. "Isn't that right, honey?"

"That's right," she agreed. But her smile was too late and too careful. "I'll give Faye a call, Sharyn. It's so good to see you again. You've changed, you know. That little-girl-lost look you had after T. Raymond died is gone. You've become a beautiful woman."

Sharyn thanked her and didn't ask them to explain their feelings about Caison. The exsenator wasn't the kind of person anyone would want to see marry a good friend. There was also the chance that George and Brenda knew more about Caison's past than she did. Everyone from their generation seemed to know about the dirty little secrets that darkened the edges of Diamond Springs.

On her way home, she called Ernie. The conversation from dinner kept gnawing at her thoughts. "Do you remember Barker Rosemont?"

"Sure," he answered. "He was a son of a gun. I haven't heard his name in years. Who asked about him?"

Sharyn told him about George coming back. "He's defending Ed. I hope that's a good thing."

"George is a good guy," Ernie reassured her. "I'm glad he's back. Was he the one remembering old Barker? He was back in his day. He probably even met the boy."

"Where do I know that name from besides the hallowed halls of the Stag?"

"I'm not sure. There are plenty of Rosemonts around. I think Barker had ten or twelve kids. His brother only had the one daughter. They had a couple sisters too. Probably prolific as well. I guess you could know them from anywhere. Maybe from school."

Sharyn shrugged, parking the Jeep outside her apartment. "You're right. Could be from anywhere. The name sounds familiar. Anything on RR Enterprises?"

"Not yet. I'm beat though and Annie says to come home."

"Do it. We can't help Ed if we drive ourselves into the ground. Have you heard anything from Joe about Ed's transfer?"

"Not a word. Think he can get it put off?"

"Maybe." She yawned. "I'm home now. I'll talk to you tomorrow."

"Okay. I hope things are looking up for Ed and Trudy tomorrow."

She agreed with him then closed her cell phone, locked her Jeep and went upstairs. She opened the door to her apartment, yawning as she sorted through her mail. Nothing but bills and sales offers. She put the mail down on her kitchen table then looked up as she heard a beep from her answering machine.

Her apartment had been ransacked. Everything was tossed around like a mini-tornado had ripped through her belongings. Pillows were slashed open. Food and dishes were tossed out of the kitchen cabinets. The refrigerator was emptied, everything was on the floor. She knew what they were looking for.

Her heart pounded as she walked around the debris until she reached her bathroom. The medicine cabinet was off the wall. The hollow behind it was empty. Her father's book was gone.

With shaking hands, she dialed Brewster's cell phone number. "Someone took the book."

He understood. "Gallagher and I will be right there."

* * *

Sharyn raged at Brewster when he finally reached her apartment. "I've kept that book safe and secret for over six months. I tell you about it and someone breaks in here and steals it. I don't know what that says for your security or your investigation. Where's Gallagher?"

"Gone." Brewster walked randomly around her apartment, viewing the damage. "I know it doesn't look good for him with all this. But he may be in trouble. We have to contain this, not let it impede the investigation."

"Contain it?" she demanded. "If Gallagher is part of the problem and gave this away, you don't have an investigation to contain. I don't care if you've spent your life trying to solve the puzzle of what goes on here. The rest of us have to live our lives. I'm going to find out who killed Duke and his mechanic."

"I don't blame you for not trusting us, Sheriff. But Gallagher could be dead. I called the bureau. They should have a team out here tonight. In the meantime, I'll call in a forensics friend I've worked with before. He'll go over everything and we might find out who did this."

Even as he said the words, Sharyn had a terrible feeling in the pit of her stomach. It wouldn't be Nick, *couldn't* be Nick. The FBI would have their own people, not a local medical examiner. "I can handle it myself, thanks."

"I know you're angry about losing your father's book. But at least you had a chance to make a copy. You didn't have that here, did you?"

"No. I wasn't that stupid. But without the original, what good is my translation? You know a judge would want both."

"Without corroborating evidence, I agree. But Gallagher has been working with the copy you gave him." Brewster stopped and looked away from her.

"Which is good if Gallagher didn't turn the whole thing over to Jack Winter," she reminded him.

"We don't know that yet. I've known Gallagher a long time. He's a good agent. I don't believe he went rogue. If anything, he probably gave his life to protect the secret."

There was a commotion at the door where Brewster had stationed two other agents. He excused himself and went to find out what was happening. Sharyn turned her back, pretending to look at a broken chicken cup on the floor. She could hear Nick's voice as he and Brewster shook hands.

"It's been a while, Nick," Brewster said. "I knew I could count on you to keep this quiet. I don't want the press or the local police involved. I'm sure you know Sheriff Howard. She's been working with us on this investigation."

"I've worked with her," Nick remarked. "But I don't know her as well as I thought."

Sharyn turned around as Brewster brought Nick into the room. She met his eyes, refusing to back down from her decision not to tell him what was going on. She could see that he was angry, probably hurt, that she hadn't trusted him. She never thought he'd find out this way.

"Sheriff, your medical examiner has worked on some important cases for us in the past," Brewster told her. "He helped us break up a counterfeiting gang in New York before he went all rural on us. I know he's done a good job for you. You can trust him with this."

"I'm sure I can," she replied. "Where do you want to start?"

Nick put down his black bag and pulled on his gloves. "Let's start where the book was stolen and work towards the door. I'll be working alone on this due to the nature of the incident. You can document for me as I go, Sheriff." He handed her his notebook and camera. "Shall we get started?"

Brewster nodded. "I'm going to leave McKinley and Forester here to make sure nothing else happens. I'm going to meet the team so we can get started looking for Gallagher. Will you be all right, Sheriff?"

"I'll be fine," she answered, still angry. "But I won't work with you anymore. This is it for me."

"I guess I don't blame you. But keep an open mind, Sheriff. We may have some other answers."

Nick was already in her bathroom when she found him. "Go ahead. Yell at me for not telling you. I did what I thought was best."

He continued dusting the empty space in the wall. "Get a picture of this, Sheriff. We'll want to document as much as we can."

"Nick, you can't ignore me. We work together. Someone might think it's strange."

"I think I found something here," he told her. "Wait. It's probably only your fingerprints."

Sharyn slammed the bathroom door, trapping them in the tiny room. "Neither one of us is leaving until we talk this out."

He stopped dusting and glared at her. "Why didn't you tell me?"

"Because it was best for you not to know. If you weren't involved, no one could accuse you of being part of it."

"That's stupid. You didn't tell me because you like keeping secrets. Maybe it's because the rest of your life is lived in front of the public."

"Don't psychoanalyze me!"

"Don't always shut me out!"

"I'm sorry. I did what I thought I should do." She looked at the camera she held instead of his face. "I wanted to tell you. I really felt like you were safer if you didn't know."

He put down his dusting brush. "For future reference, I don't care if I'm safer or not. How do you think I would've felt if they called me in tonight and you'd been here when they went through your apartment? All I ask is that you keep me in the loop."

She put her arms around him and kissed him for a long time. "I won't let it happen again. I swear you'll always know where I am and what I'm doing twenty-four hours a day."

"That may be more than I can handle." He laughed. "But if I could be in on the big stuff, I'd be happy."

"I can do that."

"Okay. Let's get going and see if we can find out who did this. I don't expect to, but you never know. Even a pro can get careless. Feel free to start at the beginning and tell me about this black book."

"After that, you have to tell me about the counterfeiting ring you helped break. I'm not the only one holding back."

"That was in the past," he reminded her. "That doesn't count."

There was a loud pounding on the door to remind them that they weren't alone. "Everything okay in there, Sheriff?" It was Brewster.

"Everything's fine. There are some fingerprints on the back of the door."

"All right. Just checking. I'm leaving now. I'll let you know what happens."

"Thanks. I'll talk to you later."

Nick shook his head. "Fingerprints on the back of the door? Couldn't you think of something better than that?"

"No. I did the best I could with the material I had." She took a picture of the back of the door. "Look. There really *is* something on here. It looks like talcum powder."

"Don't touch it. Trade places with me."

She had to climb into her bathtub to get to the other side of the bathroom. Nick was bent over the white mark on the door. "I think it might be dust from the open sheetrock where you kept the book. There's a partial print in it. Maybe we'll get lucky."

The phone rang in the bedroom. Nick opened the door and stepped aside so she could answer it. She grabbed it on the last ring before the answering machine picked up. It was Ernie. "Roy just took Trudy from her house. She called me when she saw him at her door."

"What happened?"

"They found the Glock. Some lucky fisherman found it in his boat that was tied up close to the pier where the cigarette boat came up. He hadn't gone out since then. He got in the boat tonight and found it. Roy brought Trudy in until they could test the gun. He's trying to call Nick now."

Sharyn heard the cell phone ring in her bathroom. She knocked on the door and said, "Don't answer it, Nick."

"Why not?" he demanded from the other side of the door. "It's probably important."

"It's Roy. They found Trudy's gun."

The ringing stopped and Sharyn sighed. The bathroom

door opened and Nick looked at her. "You know, I'm going to have to answer some time or they'll come and get me. One way or another, that gun is going to be tested. If it's the same one that shot Gunther, Roy will arrest Trudy. You can't stop that from happening."

"I know. Hold on." She put the phone back to her ear. "Ernie, Nick's here with me. My apartment was vandalized. He's doing the work on it. I'll meet George at the police station. Tell Trudy not to worry. We'll figure this mess out."

"I guess that means I'm on my own," Nick said.

"A fisherman found the Glock," she explained. "Roy brought Trudy in. Can you do this without me?"

"I've managed before. But thanks for the concern."

She stared into his dark eyes. "Are we okay now?"

"Will you stay if I say no?" His tone was serious but a small smile played on his lips.

"Probably not. Trudy needs me more right now. I can always find you later and make you forgive me."

"I'm just kidding. We're fine, as long as you don't lie to me again."

"I didn't lie to you. Mine was a sin of omission."

"Whatever. Don't find little black books that may get you killed without telling me."

She kissed him and smiled. "Will you come and sleep in front of my door with several guns to protect me?"

"Definitely." He kissed her then put on his heavy glasses. "Now get out of my way. You're messing up my crime scene."

"I'll call you as soon as I can. I love you, Nick."

He stared at her for a long moment. "I love you too, Sharyn. Be careful."

Sharyn waited outside for George in the cool September morning. Reporters were already gathering at the police station. They joked, half asleep, as they set up their cameras. They didn't pay any attention to her as she stood in the shadows. The reporter from the night desk at the *Gazette* made a joke about missing the sheriff because Roy was so ugly. The smell of coffee and cigarettes littered the air.

George arrived half-dressed, his hair standing up on his head. He clutched his briefcase under one arm and looked bewildered when he approached the station. Sharyn stepped out of her hiding place and took his arm.

Immediately, two reporters ran to question them. Sharyn opened the door and helped George inside. "Not now, boys."

"I'm glad you were there," George said. "I wasn't sure where to go. Are you holding Trudy or is Roy holding her?"

"Don't feel bad. Half the county is still confused and they've been here the whole time." Sharyn looked around the familiar office. A bittersweet pang of nostalgia swept over her. She pushed it aside and focused on why they were there. "Roy is holding Trudy because the crime took place inside the city limits. I handle everything in the county around Diamond Springs."

"I should've known." He tried to push his hair down with one hand. "If it would've been you, Trudy and I would still be asleep in our beds."

Sharyn didn't care for the observation. She wanted to think she'd treat her assistant like anyone else involved in a homicide. But she was so convinced Trudy wasn't responsible, he might be right. Would she have rousted her in the middle of the night to question her because they found her gun?

"Sheriff." Roy nodded to her and extended his hand to her companion. "George. It's good to see you. How have you been getting along?"

"Just fine, Roy. Thanks. Too bad we have to meet this way." George glanced around the room. "Is my client available?"

"I assume you mean Ms. Robinson. The grapevine sure talks fast, doesn't it?" Roy laughed. "I won't even ask how you knew. We got her in a cell downstairs. I'll have someone bring her up to the conference room." He studied Sharyn. "Is there something I can do for you, Sheriff?"

Once again Sharyn was caught between the law and her concern for her friend. She wasn't there in her official capacity but Trudy's friend couldn't be there when she talked to her lawyer either. She knew she was in good hands. "I'll call

Trudy's family. Let me know how it goes, George. Thanks for coming."

"My pleasure." He took her hand. "Don't worry about a thing."

She called Trudy's oldest son and told him what happened. He promised to call the rest of his family and head down to the police station. They didn't want their mother to be alone. But he also made it clear that everything happening was Ed's fault. The family didn't want her to marry him. He was nothing but a flirt and a womanizer.

Sharyn let him spout his anger and frustration. She knew it must be hard for him to see his mother in this spot, knowing how much she'd changed recently, and not blame Ed. She got off the phone with him as she reached her apartment. Nick was still busy collecting evidence. She stepped in to help him again, taking pictures and notes as they moved through her devastated home.

She told him about finding the black book, the college students who tried to help her decipher it and her final stroke of luck using her father's love of racing to find the answer to the riddle.

"That's amazing. I hope you had a copy." He bagged and labeled a hair sample that didn't look curly and red.

"I did. Two, actually. I gave one to Agent Gallagher and put one in my safe deposit box. I've worked on it all this time, Nick, and no one knew. Once I told the FBI, *this* happened. I think Gallagher is working with Jack."

"If he is," Agent Brewster broke into their conversation, "he's paid his debt. We found him at the safehouse a few miles outside the county line. We agreed to meet at that point if there was trouble. He's been shot twice in the back of the head."

"Was my book there with him?" Sharyn asked, knowing it sounded cold.

"No. The CD wasn't there either. I think if anything, the people we've been investigating found out what was going on and took the opportunity to get the information. They killed Gallagher in the process."

Sharyn got to her feet. "I'd like to believe that, Brewster. But so far, the evidence doesn't point that way. The chances are that Gallagher outlived his usefulness."

Nick collected his final sample. He yawned and stretched then his cell phone rang again. "I'm taking this back to the lab. Maybe we'll have some answers about Gallagher. I got a few clear prints from the bathroom. We'll see."

"I can send in some people to help you clean this up, Sheriff," Brewster volunteered in a heavy voice.

"Thanks anyway." She glanced around at the mess. "I'll take care of it. I think enough strangers have been in my house for one day."

There was a scuffle in the hall and one of the agents came to the door. "There's a man out here, Ernie Watkins. Says he's a friend of the sheriff."

"Let him in," Sharyn said. "I'll talk to you later, Nick."

"I'll keep my two men at your door," Brewster offered.

"I think whoever did this already got what they wanted." Sharyn leaned down and picked up a can of corn. "You can't baby-sit my place forever. I appreciate the offer but I'll be fine."

Ernie came in the door with a stunned look on his face. "What happened? And why is the FBI involved with a local problem?"

Nick picked up his bag to leave. "Just remember, she didn't tell us for our own good."

When everyone else was gone, Sharyn and Ernie sat down at her kitchen table, shards of chicken cups between them. She explained everything to him. He grimaced at a few of her ideas, especially her reluctance to tell him about the book and the FBI investigation because she felt he held things back from her.

"I'm sorry," she finished. "I wanted to tell you."

"I know. You kept it from me for my own good." He rested his head on one hand, elbows on the table. "I never thought you felt that way. You must know me well enough to know I couldn't sit on information that might have something to do with your daddy's death. Everything I ever said to you in that vein was because I was afraid for you."

She touched his hand. "Part of me realized that. Another part has always been afraid to ask too many questions. I was afraid the answers would be horrible."

"Well, you listen to me this one last time. Your daddy would never play ball with those men. He knew what was going on. He couldn't prove anything. We talked about it. I guess he got the idea of working with the FBI. It cost him his life, Sharyn. I don't know if it was worth it."

"Who can say? But I guess I have too much Howard blood in me. Aunt Selma said no to Jack and so did Dad. I don't have much choice."

"Then I guess I don't have any choice to back you up."

The phone rang and Sharyn traced the cord until she found it. "Hello?"

"Roy was waiting for me when I got here," Nick said. "It took about twenty minutes. The bullet that killed Gunther came from Trudy's gun. I'm sorry, Sharyn."

Chapter Ten

The story was ready in time for the morning reports on TV and radio: SHERIFF'S ASSISTANT ARRESTED FOR MURDER.

"Ed's gonna go berserk." Joe read the headline. "Think there's any way we can keep it from him?"

"Not unless we knock him out," Cari mourned. "And you did such a good job keeping him here for a few days too."

"He's bound to try and find some way to get her off the hook," Marvella told them. "He'll make something up and tell them he did it. He was there that night they found the boat. He knows what went on."

"We're going to have to find out what happened to both men," Sharyn said. "Just because Trudy's gun killed Gunther doesn't mean she pulled the trigger. I'd like you all to step into the conference room. Everyone's been up all night. A few more minutes won't matter very much."

"Do we get to help solve the murder?" Terry was excited by the prospect. "I'm not as old as some of you. I have a lot of stamina. I could patrol at night and work homicide during the day for a while."

Marvella frowned at him. "What are you talking about? I'm not old. And I've worked double shifts a time or two. Don't be telling me how young you are. You're still maturing. You've got a lot to learn."

They followed Sharyn and Ernie into the conference

room, still squabbling. JP, Joe and Cari came in behind them and closed the door. The room was a tight fit around the rickety table. All of them longed for their old conference room but no one bothered saying it out loud.

"I'm going to apologize beforehand for not sharing this with you," Sharyn began. "The FBI asked me to lay low on this investigation. They're working on one of their own that may be jeopardized by any revelations we have on ours. I was willing to play along until I learned that their investigation has been compromised. We all know Trudy and Ed aren't responsible for these crimes. All we have to do now is prove it."

"Sounds good, Sheriff," Terry said. "What do you want us to do?"

"If we knew that, son," Ernie replied, "there wouldn't be a problem. We're going to have to think here and find some possible angles."

"From what little I've heard," Cari offered, "the list of people who wanted to kill Duke is pretty long."

"We may have to concentrate on Gunther. He's the wild-card," Sharyn said. "Why would someone want to kill him?"

"If Trudy is right, maybe Duke killed Gunther to keep him from telling Trudy what happened to Ben." Joe polished his sunglasses on a pristine white cloth he kept in his pocket.

"But how would we prove that?" Marvella demanded. "We can't even prove what happened that night. For all we know, Trudy killed him for messing with her."

Everyone looked at Sharyn. "You're right, Marvella. What we'll have to do is piece together what happened that night. All we have now is a blank spot where Trudy is concerned."

"Someone had to see them together," Ernie said. "Either at the Stag or at the dock. I hate that Mr. Percy let Marti go. Chances are he saw something."

Joe finished cleaning his sunglasses and put them back on. "Is that the only problem? Because I can find Marti. I've done it before."

"Let's do that," Sharyn agreed. "We'll have to find some leverage to get him to talk."

"He's allergic to pain." Joe punched one gloved hand into another. "I could work on *that* allergy."

Terry's eyes gleamed. "Can I help?"

"No one is going to hurt Marti," Ernie told him.

"Not much anyway." Joe snickered. "He's kind of soft and scared. It doesn't take much."

"Stop messing with the boy, Joe." Ernie looked at Marvella. "I want you to take Terry out to the speedway. We need to pick up that videotape they said they made the day Duke was killed. Cari will go over it and see if there's anything worth looking at."

"In the meantime," Sharyn added, "JP will go with Joe to look for Marti. Ernie and I will be following up another lead. The three of you from the night shift, don't work past noon. You have to get some rest. Call it in if you find any information. Be prepared for anything. Don't take any chances."

They all left the sheriff's office with two volunteers trying to do Trudy's job. JP picked up Trudy's nameplate and kissed it before he left.

"Where are we off to?" Ernie asked Sharyn as they got in the Jeep.

"We have to go to Trudy's and look for a pink silk shirt."

He nodded. "What are we going to do with it if we find one?"

"I'm going to eat an entire gallon of chocolate ice cream and resign as sheriff," she promised. "What about you?"

"I don't know. Even if we find it, it doesn't prove she killed Gunther any more than her gun does. The evidence may be against her but it doesn't make her guilty."

"I just hope we don't find it," she said. "And I hope Roy hasn't beaten us there."

They reached Trudy's and Ed's small house about fifteen minutes later. There was no sign of Roy or any other law enforcement group. They used Ed's key to get inside. Having his permission to search the house kept them from bothering with a search warrant.

"What color pink was that?" Ernie held up a bright pink shirt a few minutes later.

Sharyn consulted the tag inside. "Nope. This is polyester. Nick definitely said silk."

They continued searching for half an hour without finding anything made out of silk. The pink polyester was as close as they came.

"I'm not surprised," Ernie told her. "We know she left wearing that white shirt and blue jeans. She'd have to change clothes while she was gone then put those three-day-old clothes back on."

Sharyn sat down beside him on the sofa. "There was definitely a pink silk fiber on the piece of window cut out. Nick said Megan made the red smudge on the rifle as lipstick. Since it involves a fashion accessory, she's probably right. We're looking for a woman as the shooter. Not Trudy. But some other woman."

"Could be an old girlfriend," he suggested. "Could be a new girlfriend."

"Could be a woman who wasn't his girlfriend."

Ernie laughed. "When a woman met Duke, she wanted him. He was a babe magnet."

She shuddered. "I'm glad I'm not a babe. But where do we go from here?"

Before he could answer, Roy and David burst into the room. "Sheriff, I think you're intruding on my investigation." Roy took off his hat and wiped his brow with a dark handkerchief. "And if I find out your boyfriend has been giving you privileged police information, I'm going to go to the commission."

Sharyn smiled. "Good luck. Nick has a special relationship with the commission. Especially Julia Richmond."

David's smug face frowned. "What do you mean?"

"Nothing." She got to her feet. "We're done here. But bear in mind, Chief, our investigation involves this house too. It'd be hard to prove what was privileged for your investigation and what was privileged for mine. See you later."

She and Ernie walked out the door, not bothering to close it after them. "Nick hasn't given you anything you shouldn't have, has he?" Ernie asked.

"I honestly don't know," she said. "You know Nick. I don't think he'd cross that line."

Sharyn's phone rang. It was George. "They arraigned Trudy and bound her over for trial with a one-hundred-thousand-dollar bond. Her son put up his house so she could get out."

"Thanks, George. You must be exhausted. I really appreciate you coming out and taking care of her." Sharyn closed her cell phone after he promised to keep her posted, and related the information to Ernie.

He smacked the door with his fist. "I can't believe this is happening. If Ed would've let Trudy take the blame for Duke's killing too, he wouldn't be in this fix. Trudy's probably going to walk away clean."

"The judge might have let her go for Gunther's death but he wouldn't have for both of them."

"I know. This whole thing is stupid. I hate feeling helpless. But there's nothing we can do. We'll have to hope the system still works."

Sharyn started the Jeep and headed back to town. "What I saw in Ed's case didn't give me much faith in our system. I hope we can do better than that."

"I haven't seen that happen yet, Sheriff. No disrespect intended. I think this may be too tough for us. Even the FBI can't figure out what's going on without losing people over it."

"What if what happened with Trudy isn't really part of the FBI's investigation?" she asked. "Maybe what we'll dig up may affect them but suppose this other part is something more personal. Like a vendetta against Duke."

"You could be right. Trudy might've got in the middle of something. Maybe it was just convenient to have her there to blame for the whole thing."

Sharyn's cell phone rang again. It was Nick. "I may have something for you but I'm working with the kids on Duke's car. Can you swing by?"

"Are you at the lab or the impound lot?"

"At the lab. Keith and Megan took the car apart yesterday. I'll see you when you get here."

"Nick thinks he has something," she told Ernie as she turned the Jeep away from the courthouse to go by the hospital.

"I sure hope it's something more than a lick and a promise. I could use some cheering up about now. You don't think Ed will do anything else stupid like try to convince people he killed Gunther too, do you?"

"I hope not." She parked next to Nick's black SUV. "I'm hoping George will keep him calm."

They walked into the basement, looking for Nick. The normal smell of the morgue mixed with the scent of gas and oil. Ernie put his hand over his nose and mouth. "This place smells worse every day. I hope it's not going to give Nick cancer or something."

"I don't think there are any smells that make people have cancer," Sharyn remarked.

"No." Nick came up behind them and draped his arm around her shoulders. "But I read on the Internet this morning that eating grits can cause problems. All of you may have to give it up."

Ernie laughed. "Yeah. Like that's gonna happen. Besides, you've got it wrong. Grits protects you from bad things happening. Look at Ed. He doesn't eat grits. Look what a mess he's in."

"It didn't keep you from getting shot a few months ago," Nick pointed out. "It's not any good unless you're putting a brick wall together."

"I didn't come here to discuss the merits of grits," Sharyn told him. "You said you had something?"

"I do. I'm sorry. I know you're busy. Find anything yet?"

"Yeah, actually we did." Ernie grinned at him. "Trudy doesn't have a single pink silk shirt to her name."

"What about Ed?" Nick asked with a crooked grin.

"I checked that," Ernie confided. "He didn't have one either. I was greatly relieved."

"Excuse me." Sharyn moved away from Nick. "You *did* say you had something to show us?"

Nick glanced at Ernie. "She's testy today. That's what

happens when you can't sleep because you're racked with guilt over not telling your significant other what's going on in your life."

"And being up all night with your apartment turned upside down and your possessions stolen." She glared at him. "You *did* say you had something to show us?"

"Yes I did." He pulled a report from his pocket. "The state crime lab wasn't as backlogged as usual, so we already know what the red smear is on the rifle." He put on his glasses and read, "Red dye number two, carmine, perfume. In other words, lipstick. Megan was right."

"Do we know what kind?" Sharyn asked, taking the report from him.

"It's not something you can buy at Eckerd's. It's only available through an exclusive spa in France. They ship it out all over the world to their clients."

"Client list?" she hoped.

"On its way," he responded. "Well, I hope it's on its way. My French is a little rusty. We're either gonna get a client list or a recipe for squishing the little red bugs they make carmine with."

"I'm glad I don't wear lipstick," Ernie said.

"Don't worry," Nick joked. "They're in lots of foods and other products. You've probably eaten them in candy and juice."

"Is that it?" Sharyn tried to bring them back. "Do you have something else?"

"I do, as a matter of fact. Step this way." Nick showed them into the lab. Megan and Keith were taking apart Duke's car seat. "They're convinced there was a second bullet," he explained to Sharyn and Ernie.

"But didn't you say there was only one wound?" Ernie asked.

"I did. They don't believe me. I think Duke was so famous around here that they have to believe it took more than one bullet to take him down." Nick crossed the room to stand beside his work table. "I found a lot of prints at your place, Sharyn. None of them were unusual. You. Ernie. Me.

Your mom. Caison. The normal people you'd expect to find there. I found an interesting partial in the bathroom, thanks to the sheetrock dust."

"Do you have a match for it?" Ernie walked around the table touching the instruments.

"Officer David Matthews." Nick looked at Sharyn as he said the name. "Is he a frequent visitor or was this a one-time thing?"

"Don't be stupid," Sharyn defended. "You know David has never been in my apartment. At least I've never *invited* him into my apartment. That whole thing he had for me right after you and I got together was only in his head. Besides, I wasn't living in this apartment then."

"I think a simple no would've sufficed," Ernie told her. "If Annie gave me all that, I'd *know* she was fooling around with David."

"Her too?" Nick shook his head. "That David. He gets all the girls. Must be the fast car and high-end lifestyle. I need a job working with Roy. Maybe I could make some real money then. Or maybe I could attract rich women like Julia Richmond. Then I'd only have to have a sheriff and a kindergarten teacher on the side."

Sharyn ignored him and sat down on the stool to look at the print that was in the microscope. "Why would David break into my apartment? How is he involved in this?"

"Maybe you should slow down and think about that some," Ernie recommended. "Are you *sure* he hasn't been over there? You've had a few parties. Maybe he was there."

She frowned at him. "I felt like I was lucky to escape with my life when he thought he was in love with me. I wouldn't invite him to a party."

Ernie shrugged. "I've known David since he was knee high to a grasshopper. He's brain dead sometimes but I don't believe he's a thief. I think he'd sneak into a party at your place he wasn't invited to, but I don't think he'd steal from you."

"His print was in the sheetrock dust from the wall where I was hiding Dad's book. He put his hand on the inside of my bathroom door," she explained. "The question isn't whether or not he was there but how did he find out about the book?"

"I can't help you with that," Nick said. "I was joking about him being there with you. I'm not *that* insecure. I sent some hair and fiber samples I found to the FBI. They're doing the autopsy and crime scene work on Agent Gallagher. I'm glad he died in another county or they'd probably want me to do it here."

"So you're in tight with the Feds, huh?" Ernie asked. "There must be something interesting about your past you're not telling us."

"And I don't plan to tell you," Nick said. "But as soon as I hear anything about those samples, I'll let you know. Gallagher may not have been in your apartment."

"You mean David did all that damage by himself," Sharyn stated flatly.

"You can't arrest him," Nick reminded her. "Your apartment is in Diamond Springs. Did you even report it to Roy?"

"No. Brewster told me not to." She got to her feet and started toward the door. "But Roy or Brewster can't keep me from taking David apart for it. Maybe you should stay here, Ernie."

"And maybe you should slow down," Ernie said. "You can't take him apart even if he *was* in your apartment. First of all, if he took the book, doesn't that put him right in the middle of this mess? Right now, that could mean he was working with Gallagher. We don't know yet if he was clean or dirty?"

She stopped. "You're right. Looking back on it, this could explain some things. David could've been our leak when he worked for the sheriff's department. Maybe that's how Jack always knew what was going on."

"You could be wrong about him too. David worked for a couple of years before T. Raymond was killed. I hate to see the look on Ed's face if David's dirty." Nick sat down on the stool Sharyn recently vacated. "But either way, you'll have to pretend like you don't know. If the FBI is investigating David, telling *him* you know this could destroy the lead they have on him."

Ernie scuffed his boot on the old green tile floor. "I always knew that boy was as dumb as a box of soda crackers even before he got involved with the Richmond family."

"I'll see what Brewster has to say," Sharyn promised. "Besides, I have a murder to solve. Two of them, if you count Gunther's. Which I suppose I have to do if we're going to help Trudy."

Nick crossed the room and drew her close to him. "I know it's not easy for you to look away from this. It's more than your job. Brewster may not be watching David. But this print confirms his involvement. If we can put Gallagher at your apartment too, they may want to pick David up and question him."

She closed her eyes and rested her head against him. "I hope so."

"Well, we better get going." Ernie coughed and glanced at Megan and Keith who were watching them. "Let us know when you have that list, Nick. In the meantime, we'll keep sniffing around."

Sharyn called Brewster and took Ernie with her to meet him. Brewster took one look at her deputy and pulled her aside. "I thought I told you no outside involvement."

"Ernie is my right hand. He knows what I know. I told you I was willing to play ball with you until all the rest of this happened. Now it's *my* show."

He looked as irritated as his mangled shirt collar. "I could pull the plug on *that* idea, Sheriff."

"And you could do this on your own," she replied, unimpressed. "You've already lost one man. I don't intend to have that happen. Ernie stays or I leave with him."

"All right. What have you got?"

She told him what Nick found. "I want to talk to David."

"Out of the question."

"So he's part of the investigation. How long have you known about him?"

"Long enough. I can't divulge that information, Sheriff. You can't talk to anyone about this investigation. It was unfortunate what happened to your apartment. But vigilante justice isn't the answer here. We're on the verge of a major breakthrough. I won't allow you to impede our process."

"Your process isn't working that well." She kept her eyes locked with his. "And I'm not a vigilante. I'm the sheriff of this county. Out of deference to Gallagher losing his life, I'll wait a while longer. But you'd better come up with some answers fast."

She got back in the Jeep, leaving Ernie to follow her. He closed the door behind him and let out a long sigh. "That was a tussle. Are you sure you want to go this way? The Feds can give you a hard time."

"Did you know my father was working with them? Brewster claims he was. The black book was definitely some kind of schedule for delivery, which goes along with the FBI's story."

"Are you telling me you don't trust the FBI now?" He worried his hat with his fingers. "I didn't know anything about your daddy working with the Feds. But that doesn't mean it didn't happen. If it wasn't for your apartment being broken into, I wouldn't know about you working with them either and I thought we were pretty tight. Brewster wears a federal badge. That's gotta mean something."

"Maybe." She waited until Brewster left to pull out of the Motel 6 parking lot where they agreed to meet. "But even he's not sure if he lost Gallagher because he was defending the code book or outlived his usefulness. Someone had to tip David and whoever helped him search my apartment."

"Nick said he was looking into that," he reminded her. "Let's not put the cart before the pony. If we find out Gallagher was there too, then we have something to deal with."

"I know you're right," she said, heading for the court-house. "But just the idea of David going through my stuff makes me want to punch him."

"I know it's gotta be creepy." Ernie shivered thinking about it. "But we have to be sure. We don't want another agent killed here."

Cari met them at the office door. "I'm glad you're here. Marvella and Terry brought the tape back from the speedway. We're about to take a look at it. Come upstairs."

They sat together in one of the judges' chambers to view the tape. Marvella was recounting how she had to threaten Spunky Tucker to get the tape. Terry enjoyed every minute of it.

"Shhh," Ernie said. "Let's watch the tape. This could be important."

"Did anybody bring the popcorn?" Marvella asked.

The tape was in black and white. Most of it was long moments of watching Duke's car go around the track. Sharyn had Cari speed up to the end. They watched the last ten minutes of Duke's final run. The car was moving smoothly down the track, accelerating along the straight-away, taking the banked turns at incredible speeds.

Sharyn saw a faint blip on the screen. "What was that?" A moment later, the sound of gunfire, the same sound she'd heard at the track, sent the number six car spinning out of control. "Can you go back? I thought I saw something on the edge of the track."

Cari used the remote to back up the tape. "I didn't see anything. Do you think it was the shooter?"

"I don't know." Sharyn sat forward to view the tape. "It seems like the timing was off for it to be the shooter. But I can't be sure."

They reached the spot on the tape again. Sharyn had Cari back up to the spot on the left side of the track. "There it is again. It looks like someone standing there."

"It could be anyone," Terry said, squinting at the TV.

"No one else was supposed to be there," Sharyn explained. "Only Duke's pit crew was inside the speedway. Can we focus in on that person?"

Cari rolled her eyes. "Only if you buy me some expensive

equipment. This is the best I can do with the tape. It looks like it could be a person or a small light fixture. It's kind of blurry."

"Yeah," Marvella agreed. "You can't tell if there's a gun or not."

"We could take it over to the college," Ernie suggested. "There's a class over there that has all kinds of equipment for this kind of thing. They might be able to help us out."

Cari moved the tape forward slowly. The sound of the gunshot was definitely after the car passed the person or thing on the side of the track. "Whoever that is could be the shooter. Although I think he or she would've been facing the back of Duke's car."

"You might be right," Sharyn agreed. "But if that isn't the shooter, he or she might know who the shooter is. Pack it up. We'll take it over to the college."

Before they could leave, a call came in from Gold Mountain. There was a disturbance in the small community about ten minutes from Diamond Springs. The local constable had called for help.

"You want us to take that?" Marvella asked Sharyn.

"No. I want you and Terry to go home and get some rest. I need you tonight. I appreciate your help and I'll let you know what happens." She looked at Cari. "Could you take this over to the college and see what you can find?"

"Sure," Cari said. "Where do I go?"

Ernie scribbled a note on a piece of paper. "It's Professor Agnew. He used to be on the second floor."

"I'll find him. You two be careful out there." Cari took the note from him.

"Are you sure you don't want us to come with you?" Marvella asked again. "It might do Terry a world of good to see something like this played out."

"Terry's better off getting some sleep," Sharyn said. "You too. I need you sharp for the nightshift. There'll be too many opportunities like this. He'll get the hang of it."

Marvella sighed but finally left the office. Terry left for

the shooting range, telling them that he was too pumped up to sleep. Sharyn and Ernie picked up their guns and hats. Ernie threw their bulletproof vests into the Jeep.

"I'll go ahead and put mine on," he told Sharyn. "Then you hang back when we get there and put yours on. No sense in taking any chances."

She pulled out of the parking lot and put on the lights and siren. "It's probably not that big a deal."

"Neither was going to Otis Fielding's farm over the summer. But I'd be dead if I wasn't wearing my vest that day."

"That was a freak happening."

"It doesn't hurt to be prepared for freak happenings." Ernie struggled into his vest as they headed towards the usually quiet community.

"We'll see what it looks like when we get there."

There were about twenty-five hundred people in Gold Mountain. Most of the adults worked at a small mill that made ladies underwear. The town still had a drive-in movie that had been there since the fifties. There was Fred's Diner that served breakfast and lunch. Arlie's Burgers took over for dinner. A park in the center of town was newly repainted and a red caboose was installed, donated by the railroad museum in Spencer. It was a quiet place where generations of people had raised their children, walked the tree-lined sidewalks, and been laid to rest in the local cemetery.

The trouble came, as it did to other small towns in the southern Piedmont, when the mill announced it was going to close. People grumbled and complained but they thought another buyer would come through as they had before. But this time, the mill closed for good. People went in for the morning shift and found the gates closed and padlocked. Sixty workers stood outside, pushing at the gates. They took their shotguns out of their pickups and were demanding entrance to the mill.

Sharyn stopped the Jeep and looked at the crowd. "Wasn't I the one who told Marvella and Terry to go home because we could handle it?"

Ernie handed her the vest from the back seat. "I told you. You never know what's going to happen."

The local constable responsible for keeping the peace inside the town limits recognized Sharyn's Jeep and ran over to them. "This is a mess, Sheriff. I tried talking sense to them. They won't listen. A lot of them are close to retirement. Where are they gonna get new jobs?"

"I don't know." Sharyn put on her vest and took out her riot stick. "But standing out here shooting at the gate won't help. Have you had any casualties?"

"The guard who was standing in front of the gate got knocked down. But he only got a sprained wrist. I don't know how long that's gonna last."

"Is anyone inside the building?"

"No. The owner is in Florida. He wanted to sell the place but there were no buyers. Everything's gone overseas now."

"Okay. We'll see if we can convince them to go home. I'd appreciate it if you could stay here in case we have to call in more help. But stay out of the way. I don't want anyone hurt."

Sharyn and Ernie elbowed their way to the front of the group. With their backs against the chain link fence, they tried to get the crowd's attention. Nothing seemed to permeate their frenzy to get into the mill. Ernie held up his rifle and fired a shot into the clear blue sky.

Chapter Eleven

"It's time to go home!" Sharyn shouted, trying to be heard by the entire group. "Someone is going to get hurt out here and I know none of you want that."

"But he promised the mill would stay open!" one man yelled at her. The others agreed with him.

She climbed up on the wood crate beside her. "I know your jobs are gone. I know you're wondering what's going to happen to you. But the answers aren't here."

"Where are the answers, Sheriff?" another man shouted.

"I'm sure they're with the Employment Security Commission and Social Services for now," she answered. "But if you really want to make some difference, get all of the workers from this mill and take a bus up to Raleigh. Send letters to your congressmen. If you're angry, tell people who matter. Get on TV. Talk about it on the radio. But you can't stand here with your guns and think it will make any difference."

"Nothing makes any difference," a voice said from the crowd. "The mills are closing everywhere. I'm too old and sick to learn a new trade. Who cares about me, Sheriff? What difference can I make?"

Sharyn drew a deep breath. "I'm not sure. But even if you get in the mill, what will you do? Put in a full day for no pay? The jobs are gone. The mill is closed. You should all

153

find the real answers to your problem. Go home before someone gets hurt and the only answer is for me to arrest all of you for trespassing. That won't help anyone."

The crowd was quiet for a moment. Then they started talking and moving away. Ernie sighed, watching them back off. His finger on the trigger of the rifle had begun to ache.

"Maybe that did the trick," Sharyn whispered.

He was about to answer when a bullet whizzed between them, shattering the lock on the gate. A man with a rifle stood his ground, his eyes fixed on them, daring them to do something about his act of defiance. The crowd looked back and spread out when they heard the sound. They paused, not moving, waiting to see what Sharyn would do.

"Now I know how an elephant feels," Ernie said as they drove back to Diamond Springs. In the back of the Jeep were the shooter and two other people from the crowd.

As soon as the group saw the lock was off the gate, they surged forward. Guns firing, angry voices raised, they pushed through Sharyn and Ernie and spilled into the mill.

"Human stampedes might be worse." She wiped blood from her lip as she drove. "It's lucky you got off that other shot. It kept most of them back."

"If that's luck"—he carefully moved his arm that had been stepped on by several people—"you can keep it. I thought we were gonna have to bring the whole blamed mess of them in. I was surprised when most of them turned back."

Sharyn glanced at her face in the rearview mirror. She probably had a black eye, definitely a bruise on her cheek, and a swollen lip. Standing on the crate seemed like a good idea at the time. Her aching back was there to tell her that the higher up you are, the further you fall when a large group of people pushes past you. "It's hard. I don't really blame these people for being upset. No one ever expects their life to change that dramatically."

"Yeah. People go along every day not realizing how fast it can all be taken away from them. We see more of that than most people, I guess."

Sharyn's cell phone rang. It was Joe. He and JP managed to find Marti Martin and bring him in. They were waiting for her at the office. "Thanks, Joe. Send JP home. He needs to get some sleep."

"Let's hope Marti knows something," Ernie said when she told him the news. "Otherwise his lawyer is probably going to sue us for harassment."

"I think we need to question him before Mr. Percy knows we have him."

"You think he's involved with this?"

"I don't know. He was in a hurry to let him go."

Ernie didn't want to think badly of the DA. "Percy has always been there for any vet who needed him. It doesn't matter what time it is or what he's done. I don't think he'd stoop that low."

"Ernie, Marti isn't a vet. And Mr. Percy was with Jack in the courtroom to intimidate Caison. I don't think we can trust him."

"But we trust *Caison* now? That man was as thick as thieves with Jack until Jack turned on him. I'd put my faith in Mr. Percy before I'd trust Caison Talbot."

"I thought you said it was okay for Mom to marry him?"

He scratched his head. "That's different."

Sharyn realized this was a subject they were never going to agree on. At least not unless Mr. Percy was caught doing something he shouldn't. Ernie had dubious heroes for a deputy sheriff. As far as she was concerned, Duke and Percy walked a fine line between being legitimate and being in prison.

They reached the courthouse and gave their prisoners to the jail guards. Sharyn was eager to talk to Marti.

Joe was enjoying himself by intimidating his prisoner in the conference room. Marti cringed sufficiently every time Joe growled at him. He looked up when he saw Sharyn, launching himself at her feet when she stood in the doorway. "He's a maniac!" he told her. "Someone needs to tell him the Geneva Convention gave prisoners certain rights."

"You aren't a prisoner of war, you moron," Joe said.

"Did he beat you?" Ernie asked, frowning. "Did he torture you in some way?"

"He didn't beat me exactly," Marti answered. "But he drove really fast getting here and he's been staring at me from behind those dark glasses ever since his partner left. I want to file a complaint."

Sharyn motioned for him to sit back down at the table and sat opposite him. "I only have one problem with that. I need you to answer some questions for me. After that, you can file a complaint against Deputy Landers if you want to."

Marti eyed Joe cautiously. "Shouldn't he leave the room?"

"After you answer my questions," she promised. "I need to know what happened the night Gunther was killed. And you mentioned Duke's partners at the Stag. I need to know their names."

"Sure!" He sat back in his chair and laughed. "I can give you those answers, Sheriff. Not like I want to keep living or anything. Didn't you notice that Duke didn't die in his sleep of old age? He was murdered right there in front of you! Someone like me they'd probably just drown in the lake!"

Joe leaned forward. "Like the runt of the litter?"

Marti screeched and moved back. Ernie went to stand behind his chair and pushed him towards the table. "The sheriff said she needs you to answer some questions, son," Ernie told him. "I think you better answer them."

Marti laughed again but this time it was a scared, uncertain sound. He focused on Sharyn. "I can't tell you those things. People would want to kill me more than usual. I don't know a lot about Duke's private affairs. He didn't trust me that much."

"That's too bad." Sharyn frowned at him and shook her head. "I can't help you if you don't work with me."

"You're not being smart here, son." Ernie put his hands on Marti's shoulders.

"All right. All right! Not that it will do you any good to know." He paused and studied the thin metal of the folding table, following it with his chewed fingernails. "Trudy didn't kill Gunther. He drugged her, brought her into the Stag. I don't know what he had in mind to do with her but he never got the chance. Duke went out in the boat with him. I saw him come back alone about an hour later. He was soaking wet. He made me get him some whiskey and a towel."

"Are you saying Duke killed his own mechanic?" Ernie's grip on Marti's shoulders tightened. "Why would he do something like that?"

"I don't know. Gunther had been talking to Trudy. It's not like we didn't know who she was. She might've thought everyone out there was too drunk to know she was Ben's wife but we knew."

"Did that make some difference?" Sharyn asked.

"Maybe Duke was afraid he'd give something away. Duke was the one who fixed that car and caused Ben's accident, you know. Some friend of his asked him to do it. I'm not sure who. Duke did lots of little favors for people. That's what made him so popular . . . and hard to bring down. He knew where all the bones were buried."

"So you're saying Duke killed Ben and Gunther." Ernie folded his arms across his chest. "A dozen witnesses saw him drinking at the Stag before Ben's accident."

"If Duke would've asked, the Governor would've said he was there with him." Marti rubbed his hands together. "As for Gunther, all I know is what I saw."

"Did anyone else see Duke and Gunther that night?" Sharyn asked.

"Half the people in the Stag. I could give you some names."

"That doesn't really prove anything," Joe told him. "Just because he was wet and came back alone doesn't make him a murderer. Don't you have any other information?"

Marti seemed to consider his options again. "I heard him talking to his partner about it when he came back. Does that count?"

"Who is his partner?" Sharyn asked again.

"I don't know her name. I haven't ever seen her face. Whoever she is, she's really careful. She comes in a few times a week and takes over Duke's office. I'm sure if he could've killed her as easy, he'd have done it. He hated that woman. He'd only been partners with her the last two years. He had a cash flow problem a while back and she bailed him out."

"And you heard Duke confess to his partner that he killed Gunther?" Sharyn looked up from her notes. "What did she say?"

"She said it was a good thing." Marti shrugged. "She said Gunther served his purpose and was a liability."

"If Duke already had Trudy, why didn't he just put her in the boat with Gunther?" Ernie demanded. "Why bother putting her pocketbook in the boat?"

"I wondered the same thing," Marti said. "But his partner wanted to do something with Trudy. I heard her tell Duke she had something else planned. I didn't know what until I heard Duke was killed and Trudy was there. Then I knew. That's when I knew I better run. She was bound to come looking for me."

"But you have no idea who this woman is?" Sharyn tapped her pencil on the table. "Did you notice what kind of car she drove to the Stag? Was anyone ever with her? Anything we could use to ID her could save your life if we let you go."

"Believe me, Sheriff, if I could've figured out anything about her, I would've. You can't be in my line of work and not know the people around you. It's dangerous. I needed to know just to have something over Duke. I know a few things about her. She always drove a different, expensive car. She wore something that covered her completely. A cape or something with a hood. I never talked to her, just listened through the door when Duke talked to her."

"What about her voice?" Joe questioned. "What kind of voice did she have?"

Marti thought about it. "She sounded smart, you know? Like she taught school or something."

"Did she sound like she was from around here?" Ernie asked.

"She sounded southern but smart. Not like a hick or something. She always drank Perrier when she came. Duke kept it in stock for her. She never touched whiskey. That was one reason Duke said he couldn't trust her. But that's all I know about her. Well, that and she killed Duke."

Joe leaned forward again. "You saw her do it?"

"No. Not exactly. But it makes sense, doesn't it?" Marti looked at each of them. "She wanted to do something else with Trudy and the next thing you know, Duke is shot dead and Trudy is found there with the rifle."

They left him in the conference room and stepped outside the door. Cari joined them as they talked about what Marti told them.

"Makes sense why we found Duke's wallet in the glove compartment on the boat." Joe shrugged. "He forgot he had it with him and didn't want it to get wet when he swam back. He knew Roy would assume it was there from another outing. It *was* Duke's boat."

"Yeah but all we have is sleazebag Marti's testimony that it happened at all." Ernie put his hands on his hips as he stared at the conference room door. "He could've done it himself. It's not like Duke can refute his testimony."

"You're right, Ernie," Sharyn said. "Let's get the names of the other people he said saw Duke leave with Gunther and come back wet and alone. Chances are Nick couldn't get anything else off the boat that could be useful since it was Duke's boat. We may be stuck using Marti's statement and backup testimony from other witnesses."

"What about the mystery woman?" Joe asked. "Think she's real?"

"I don't know. Marti said she took over Duke's office at the Stag when she was there. Maybe we'll go out there and see what we can find. Nick hasn't had a chance to go out there yet. Just because she was smart enough to think about hiding her face doesn't mean she thought about fingerprints. Cari, bring your fingerprint kit."

"What about me?" Ernie asked.

"I need someone out on patrol," she told him, touching a

finger to her sore lip. "But be careful, huh? This day hasn't gone very well so far. Don't take any chances."

"What do you want to do with Marti?" Joe nodded towards the conference room. "If we lock him up Mr. Percy might let him go again."

"Let's keep him here for a while," Sharyn decided. "He's not going anywhere. Maybe when we get back we'll have enough supporting evidence that we can keep him as a material witness. Mr. Percy couldn't argue with that."

"No," Joe agreed. "But he could tell anyone who wanted to kill the little creep where to find him."

"We'll deal with that when we get there. Right now, this is all we can do." Sharyn put on her hat and gun. "Let's bring in anyone Marti names as witnesses from the Stag. We'll be back as soon as we go over Duke's office."

Duke's office was cramped and crowded. It looked like it had been laid out in the 1970s. Imposing metal file cabinets filled one whole wall. Yellowed, pull-down blinds sealed the inside away from prying eyes. The lime-green shag carpet was painfully clean compared to the rest of the nightclub. A glitter disco ball was attached to the light in the ceiling.

"Wow!" Cari switched the light on and watched the refractions on the ceiling and walls. "He lived in style, didn't he?"

Sharyn stood beside a gold-plated office chair with the number six emblazoned in red. "Yeah. He lived the high life."

The walls were littered with plaques and trophies from his visits to victory lane. The photos were all of Duke with various speedway queens, an open bottle of champagne in one hand and a woman in the other. Always wearing his trademark cowboy hat and dark glasses, he cut a celebrity swath through the past thirty years. The press was bound to miss his face.

"Where do you want me to start?" Cari asked, pulling on her gloves. "What are we looking for?"

"Anything the mystery woman might've touched," Sharyn said. "The only thing we know about her is that she sounded educated and she drank Perrier."

"Yuck." Cari shuddered. "Obviously an older mystery woman. None of my friends drink that stuff anymore."

Sharyn didn't comment. She started with Duke's desk. The drawers were locked, but she found a spare key taped to the underside of the desk. She found a few other things down there as well. Two pistols, three knives and a sawed-off shotgun were duct-taped where he could reach them quickly if he needed to. She put them in plastic bags and confiscated his trashcan to take them back to the lab.

As she was about to empty the trash on the floor, she noticed an empty Perrier bottle. Using a pen she found on the desk, she picked up the bottle and put it into a plastic bag. Maybe the mystery woman drank from that bottle? She couldn't imagine Duke drinking water. She peered closely at it. There was a hint of red on the open top. Better and better.

There was another interesting piece of garbage under the water bottle. It was a letter from Richmond Enterprises confirming their sponsorship of Duke's race car for the next two years. Sharyn bagged that too.

The names of Duke's sponsors were legion, according to his records. The car sported aver a hundred stickers from the expensive one that covered the hood to a few the size of baseballs. The largest stickers denoted the sponsors who were willing to pay a few million dollars to promote their product. According to the letter, the Richmond family was going to invest heavily in racing.

"I found a few cold Perrier bottles in the freezer. They have prints on them." Cari held open the door to the mini-fridge that was shaped like a wheel. "Maybe she touched them as she browsed. There's some Brie in here too. It seems a little classy for Duke."

"Bag all of them," Sharyn said. "If Nick can get us some DNA from them, we might have some luck proving who the mystery woman is."

"Yeah, but he has to have some idea of who to look at." Cari bagged the Brie. "We don't have any idea of who she is yet."

"Maybe we'll get lucky and find a fingerprint we can use. A fingerprint that's listed somewhere." Sharyn added some loose paper and pens she found on the desk. Her eyes followed along the desktop, looking for anything that might help them find the woman.

At the edge of one glass ashtray, in the center of which was a smiling picture of Duke, was a small cigarette butt. It was very thin and tinged with dark pink lipstick. Sharyn carefully bagged it then began to dust for prints at that end of the desk. There were several clear prints but dozens of smudged ones. Maybe they'd get lucky.

When they were finished, Cari and Sharyn walked out of the office with two trashcans full of potential evidence. Two workers in hard hats and a brown-haired man in an expensive business suit were standing inside the nightclub looking at the fixtures.

"Mr. Michaelson," Sharyn hailed the ex-ADA of Diamond Springs. Alan Michaelson was working for Eldeon Percy's old law firm now. "Good to see you again. This place is off limits. We're investigating a murder."

Michaelson drew out a piece of paper. "Good to see you again, too, Sheriff. I'm sure you'll find everything in order. Judge Dailey has ruled that the Stag-Inn-Doe is not part of your murder investigation since nothing happened here."

Sharyn glanced at the legal notice. "Nothing to do with Mr. Percy, right?"

"Of course not, Sheriff. You know Mr. Percy gave up his interest in the firm when he became DA. Anything else would be illegal." He smiled. "I represent the new owner of this establishment."

"And that is?"

"I'm not at liberty to divulge that information." He smiled again.

"I'm sorry, Mr. Michaelson, but if this nightclub has already changed hands, that might be considered a motive for killing Mr. Beatty. Your client has become part of my investigation too. So you can either tell me now or I'll ask Judge Dailey to find out for me."

The lawyer stopped smiling. "I can't believe you'd consider this dive as a motive for killing somebody. You're bluffing."

It was Sharyn's turn to smile. "Maybe. You can wait to see my hand. But by then, your client will be even more suspect. The Stag probably produces pretty good revenues, wouldn't you say, Cari?"

Cari nodded, her hand on her weapon. "I'd say so. Enough that someone might kill for it. And that's what gets reported. Who knows what it makes on the side?"

The lawyer pulled out his cell phone. "I'll call my client. But I don't expect him to change his mind."

"What do we do now?" Cari asked in a whisper when the lawyer turned his back to them and crossed the room.

"Get on the phone and call for a search warrant for the whole club. Mr. Percy got one for the office. We found potential evidence there. Tell him there may be more in the club. I'll stall for time."

Cari walked back into the office. Sharyn waited while the lawyer had a heated debate on the phone. Apparently, his client was reluctant to be named. She looked around the club, wondering what changes a new owner would bring. It couldn't be worse.

"Sheriff, my client is sorry for the mix-up and certainly wants to cooperate." The oily smile was back when Michaelson approached her. "He wants no misunderstanding about the situation. The Stag is actually part of his inheritance. Mr. Beatty won it in a poker game but had no wish to keep it from the family forever. He left it in his will that the nightclub would revert back to the family at the time of his death. My client is simply following the law."

"That's fine," she said. "And who did you say your client is?"

"Arthur Rosemont. It's a matter of legal documentation. You'll find everything is in order at the courthouse."

"I'm so sure." Sharyn racked her brain over the Rosemont

name again. She knew about the connection to the nightclub but felt sure there was more. She just couldn't put the two things together.

Cari came out of Duke's office and nodded at her. Sharyn gave the lawyer his documentation back. "It seems we have a clash of interest, sir. In this case, the murder investigation wins out. We've been granted a search warrant for the entire premises. You can't touch anything until we finish our investigation."

The lawyer looked dumbfounded. "My client isn't going to be happy about this. I hope you know what you're doing. Other law enforcement officials have been sued for making mistakes."

She held the front door open for them. It wasn't easy since Marti had only wired it in place. "I'll keep that in mind. We'll let you know when you can bring your workers back in."

When they were gone, Cari sighed. "So does that mean Arthur Rosemont was Duke's partner that Marti was so afraid of?"

"Not unless Arthur is a woman's name." Her cell phone rang. "Sheriff Howard."

"Ed's going to be shipped out to the county jail this afternoon," Joe told her without waiting. "There's nothing else I can do."

Sharyn told Cari what happened when she closed her cell phone. There was nothing else to do but keep searching for the answers. "What about that tape from the speedway?"

Cari shrugged. "The professor didn't have time to look at it. I have to take it back over there."

"Maybe he'll have time today. Let's do that after we drop this stuff off at the morgue." Sharyn put a padlock and a notice on the door to the nightclub. She wished it was permanently closed but unless they found something against Arthur Rosemont that would keep him from operating the place, business would go on as usual. She kicked the broken door into place and got in the Jeep.

Nick was making his case before the county commission when they got to the lab, hoping to get a new medical examiner's van. Sharyn left the evidence and a note with Megan and Keith. "I've got the Stag padlocked. If you need to go out there, give me a call."

"What are we looking for, Sheriff?" Keith started sifting through the trash cans.

"We're looking for the prints of a mystery woman who might be involved in our double homicide. The Perrier bottle might be the best place to start."

Megan came in and put on her lab coat. "What about this ciggy, Sharyn? Looks like we've got a match on that lipstick. How many women in this area could afford that kind of gloss?"

"That's right." Sharyn smiled at her. "You've got an eye for fashion."

"It's my life. At least, looking at it is my life. I'll see if it matches what we found on the rifle."

Diamond Springs College was right next door to the hospital. With parking at a premium, Sharyn and Cari decided to walk to the professor's office. It was still cool and wet with just a hint of frost on the ground. The smell of wood smoke from fireplaces and stoves hung on the calm air. Fog shrouded the Uwharries in a wreath of ancient mystery.

Sharyn shivered despite her heavy uniform. Aunt Selma called it the goose crossing your grave. She knew there was an adequate scientific reason for it. But many times she preferred the folklore. Maybe it was the way she was raised. Maybe it was the presence of the generations before her who inhabited the mountains. Sometimes late at night, she could almost hear their voices in the wind that blew off Diamond Mountain.

"The professor is a little quirky," Cari was telling her. "Maybe you can impress on him how important this is. He didn't seem very interested in helping."

"We'll see." Sharyn pulled herself back from the lure of the mountains.

Professor Agnew was finishing a class when they arrived. He was a young man, barely thirty, with Einstein-like hair and large black-rimmed glasses. He wore a white lab coat and black rubber gloves that went to his elbows. "Are you back again?" he snapped at Cari. "I looked at your silly tape. What do you want me to say? If the quality was any worse, we'd shoot it to put it out of its misery."

Sharyn stepped forward. She was several inches taller than the professor and not above using her height and uniform to intimidate him. "I'm Sheriff Howard, Professor. We need to identify the person standing on the side of the track. Can you help us?"

He started at her belt buckle and followed a straight line up her shirt to her face. "Why didn't you say so? I've heard of you, Sheriff. It's hard to pick up the paper and not know your name. Is this related to your recent murder case?"

Cari rolled her eyes. "I *told* you it was."

"Never send a soldier to do a general's work," the professor quipped, setting up his equipment. "I believe I saw that figure sixteen-point-two minutes into the tape. Let's just look there, shall we?"

Sharyn sat on a wood stool beside him. "You have quite a memory."

"Thank you. I'm also skilled in fencing, aikido and chess. I suppose Nick wouldn't appreciate my telling you this, but I don't see a ring on your hand. That looks like an open field to me."

Sharyn could see the look of surprise on Cari's face. She smiled at the professor. "I appreciate the offer, sir. But my relationship with Dr. Thomopolis is committed if not formal."

The professor slapped the side of the cabinet he was working on. "That's the way it always is. You meet a woman you know could be interesting but she's already taken. Do you know what the ratio of men to women is in this area?"

"No. Not really." Sharyn watched the images on the tape flying by.

"And you're the sheriff?" he asked in disbelief. "I'm surprised you don't know everything about this county." He stopped the tape abruptly. "There it is. Exactly sixteen-point-two minutes. There's your shadowy figure."

Sharyn squinted at it. "Can you enhance that?"

"I suppose so. What would be the point in all this if I couldn't?" The professor used his equipment to isolate the single image. He transferred it to his computer and they went to look at it there. Enlarged, the image was even worse. Except for the dark and light pixels, it was impossible to tell anyone was there. "We should be able to adjust for the abysmal photography."

"If we could zoom in on the face," Sharyn pointed, "that's what we need."

"Of course." The professor used a program that high-lighted the area they were looking at. "Do you think this might be the killer?"

"No," Sharyn confided. "The shot came after the car passed this figure. The bullet came through the windshield. But this person probably saw who fired that shot."

Using the computer to enhance the image, the face of the person on the side of the track when Duke was killed began to get clearer. Dark hair grew away from a high forehead. A sloping nose and flat cheekbones worked down to a wide mouth and pointed chin.

"David?" Cari identified him. "Is that David?"

Chapter Twelve

"**I** don't know what you're talking about." David sat at the conference table in the sheriff's office with his hands folded behind his head, leaning back in his chair.

"And I protest *again* at you questioning my officer." Roy raised his voice loud enough to be heard outside the tiny closed space.

Sharyn put the image the professor printed for them on the table where both men could see it. "They were taping speed trials on the car. This picture was taken by a member of Duke's pit crew. He wasn't *trying* to take your picture, David. You just happened to be there."

David glanced at the picture but if he was agitated in any way, he didn't show it. "That could be anybody. You can't blame the murder on me because of this picture."

Roy looked at the image and scratched his chin. "It does look a lot like you, boy. Are you sure you don't know anything about this?"

"I swear, Chief, I don't know what she's talking about." David smiled at Sharyn. "But she's wanted some kind of revenge against me ever since I dumped her. You can't blame a woman for being spiteful sometimes."

Roy chuckled, his belly jiggled. "He's got you there, Sheriff. What's this all about?"

"I tried to explain to you when you first came in but you

168

didn't want to listen." She sat down at the table. "We retrieved a tape from Duke's pit crew. It shows David standing alongside the track as Duke's car goes by. Seconds later, the shot is fired that pierced Duke's windshield and killed him."

Roy laughed. "Then you got squat. If the car was already past David when Duke was shot in front, you can't accuse the boy of killing him."

"You're right," she agreed. "And I don't plan to. But David was there only a few yards from where it happened. He *saw* something."

Roy acknowledged her claim with a grunt and turned to his officer. "Tell the sheriff what you know."

David looked bewildered. "I don't know anything. That picture may look like me but it's not. I wasn't near the track when that happened."

Sharyn nodded. "Okay. Where were you?"

"I was working. The chief sent me out on patrol. I don't know where I was exactly at the time this happened, but I was in town. Not at the racetrack."

"In that case, you won't mind talking to the security guard from the gate at the speedway." Sharyn got to her feet again. "I brought him in to ID the person he let through the gate before me. He said it was someone in law enforcement. I thought it was Ed or Ernie but they didn't come in until after I got there."

David stuck his chin out. "I don't care who you bring in. I wasn't there."

Sharyn brought in the security guard who'd been waiting in the office. As soon as he saw David, he smiled. "That's him all right. He came in right before you, Sheriff."

"That doesn't count," Roy said. "It wasn't even a proper lineup. He was predisposed to identify my officer."

Sharyn thanked the security guard and sent him back out to the office. She closed the door to the conference room and sat down opposite David again. He was finally starting to get a little edgy. What was he hiding? Or maybe the question should be *who* was he hiding? "I think this man would pick you out of a lineup, David. He already ID'd the blue police car. What's the problem? You weren't supposed to be out there. You're afraid the chief will fire you. Talk to me. All I need to know is what you saw besides Duke's car."

David hung his head. "Okay. I was out there watching the car. I heard about Duke's new engine and I wanted to see it for myself before I put any money on it during the race." He looked at the Chief. "I'm sorry. It was only a few minutes."

Sharyn was astonished. "Since when are you interested in racing? You weren't when you worked for me."

"Things change, Sharyn." His voice was quiet as he stared into her eyes.

Roy covered his eyes with his hands. "And what else did you see while you were out there?"

"Nothing. I was watching the car. I heard a shot and got out of there before everything went crazy. I didn't want you to know I was out there. But I didn't see anything."

"How could you miss someone sticking the barrel of a rifle out of an office window a few yards from where you were standing?" Sharyn demanded, not believing him.

"I don't know." David shrugged. "I was watching the car. I wasn't looking around. I don't know how it happened."

Roy glanced at Sharyn. "We both know this boy, Sheriff. And I tell you frankly, I wouldn't have hired him except I was taking him away from you. But now that I know him, I can see why you didn't mind letting him go. If he says he was only watching the car, I believe him. It's a long shot that he might have noticed something else. But it was a good try."

"I'm not giving up that easy, Chief." She stared at David. "He might not seem too bright but he's well trained. He saw what went on that day. He knows who pulled that trigger and tried to set Trudy up. I think it was a woman who was working with Duke. I don't have a clue to her identity. At least not yet. I found some personal effects at the Stag that might help us."

"And I think you'd do anything to prove that Trudy Robinson isn't guilty of this crime," the chief rebutted her. "I talked with Martin this morning after I got your memo. He's pathetic, but he tells a good story. I don't like not having a suspect. You better have something else to back that up."

"I've got Joe out looking for Marti's witnesses from the club," she replied. "I suppose I should've sent you the list of names but I thought we'd take the next step for you. Trudy didn't commit that crime."

Roy lumbered to his feet. "You may be right, Sheriff. But you've already told us that you don't like David for it either. I suggest you work harder on your own investigation and leave mine alone. The boy is coming with me. Next time you want to talk to him, you'll have to talk to his lawyer. Come on, David."

Sharyn watched them go. The chief was right. She couldn't hold David. It was even possible he didn't see anything at the track. Or if he did, he didn't realize what he saw. Either way, there was nothing she could do.

Ernie was coming in from a quiet patrol. Joe was bringing in two of the men on Marti's list who backed his story about Duke. Sharyn might have saved Trudy, but Ed's life was still messed up. They had to find this mystery woman. And she had to learn about Arthur Rosemont.

"Cari, find Arthur Rosemont." Sharyn went to her desk. "I want to have a word with him."

"Okay." Cari answered the phone. "It's Nick. Line two."

Sharyn picked up at her desk. "Hi. Did you get any new information at the commission meeting?"

"Julia's still in my court," he replied. "She told the commission they should approve my request. Then she asked me out for lunch. I like her better every time I see her."

"That's great. I've got Megan and Keith working on some stuff we picked up at the Stag. Megan said we have another lipstick sample from a cigarette butt."

"I'll get back there as soon as I can," he said. "You know I'd rather work with cigarette butts and whatever else you picked up out there than have lunch with a beautiful, rich woman."

Sharyn laughed. "I know. That's the scary part. Where are you going?"

"She's taking me out to the Palmer Hotel. It's nice to have friends with money. What are you doing?"

"Trying to keep Ed off that county jail bus this afternoon. Lucky for me I don't have any rich friends who want to buy me lunch. Give me a call when you get back to the morgue."

"You aren't jealous, are you?"

"Nope." She smiled. "Did you want me to be?"

"It would've been nice. You've got plenty of men hanging out after you. I just wanted you to know that there might be some woman who wants to go out with me."

"Tell me about it after she sees your apartment. Then I'll be jealous."

He laughed. "It's a deal. I see Julia coming from the commission room. Talk to you later."

Sharyn put down the phone and glanced up at Cari who'd been standing beside her desk for most of her conversation with Nick. There was no privacy in their cramped, temporary quarters. "What's up?"

"I found Arthur Rosemont." Cari held out the sheet of paper. "His real name is Arthur but his friends call him Skeeter."

The name snapped in Sharyn's mind. "Skeeter and Amanda Rosemont. Julia Rosemont Richmond's parents. Look up Margaret Rosemont's husband and see how he died. I'll bet he's Barker Rosemont, the one George said lost the Stag to Duke."

"What's happening?" Ernie asked as Cari went to look up the information.

Sharyn told him what was going on. "I think we might have something here. That's definitely David in that picture. Julia has been spending a lot of time with him. Her father is taking over the Stag as it reverts back to the family. Duke killed her uncle. I think Julia could be involved in this. She might be our mystery woman. She might even be our shooter."

Ernie took off his hat and sat down in a chair near her desk. "I go out on one patrol and right away, things start falling apart. You can't accuse Commissioner Richmond of killing Duke and setting Trudy up to take the blame. Why would she do it? The Richmond family could buy the Stag any time, a hundred times. Why bother killing Duke?"

"Family pride or something more," Sharyn suggested. "Someone has been trying to kill Duke, according to the things that Trudy found out. It might *just* be a family feud. Or it might be a link to the power structure in Diamond Springs. Why didn't the FBI want us to investigate this case too closely? Who were they afraid I would spook?"

"But the Richmonds? That's asking for trouble. Besides Julia being the best commissioner we've ever had."

"I don't know, Ernie. I hope I'm wrong. If I could get a sample of her lipstick, it might match what we already have. Maybe we can get some details after that."

"How do you plan to do that?"

"Nick is having lunch with her right now. Maybe he can think of some way to get a sample."

His eyes widened. "Are you sure you want to do that?"

"It's the only way I can think of to find out the truth," she answered, getting up from her desk. "I'll see you later."

"What do you want me to do?"

"Joe is on his way in with Marti's witnesses. Take them to the police station and you and Roy hash this thing out. Get Trudy out of jail."

"Yes, ma'am. Could I put an end to hunger and achieve world peace at the same time?"

Sharyn raised her eyebrow. "Just do it. Let's wrap this thing up."

Ernie chuckled. "Feeling a mite peaked today, Sheriff?"

"Feeling like there's too much going on behind the scenes to appreciate the play, Deputy. I'll let you know what I find out."

Sharyn called Nick then waited in the busy kitchen. She hoped he could improvise enough to get what they needed. This might be their only opportunity to surprise Julia. The only other route would be more direct. But a warrant for the commissioner's lipstick would cause a stir she hoped to avoid. And if Julia wasn't guilty, she didn't want to alienate her.

"You couldn't stand it, could you?" Nick's voice interrupted her thoughts. "I can't believe you didn't trust me to have lunch with Julia. You had to sneak over here and spy on me." He laughed and put his arms around her. "I love it! I never knew you had a jealous bone in your body."

Sharyn stepped away from his impassioned embrace. "I wasn't jealous. I'm on the job. Did you get it?"

He held out a glass with frosted pink lipstick on the rim. "What's going on? What do you think Julia did?"

She quickly outlined her theory. "I'm sorry. Don't be disappointed. I *was* worried about the two of you. I worry about some other woman snatching you up all the time. Mostly, it's Megan. I know the two of you appreciate the same things in life."

Nick put his hands in his pockets. "Nice try! You don't have to lie to make me feel better. I think you're wrong about Julia. But just in case, I need to close this deal on the new van. She's still a commissioner right now and she still likes me. It could change if what you think is true."

"Close the deal." Sharyn kissed him as she put the glass in a plastic bag. "I'll talk to you later."

"Sharyn," he stopped her, "you *do* think about me once in a while even when you're working, right? You don't just love me because I help you solve crimes."

She smiled. "Of course not. Don't be silly. I think about you every time I pick up the phone to call the morgue. You're always on my mind."

"That's what I was afraid of," he muttered before he went back into the dining room.

Sharyn dropped the glass off with Megan, who promised to have an analysis in a few hours. Then she called the office. Cari located Arthur 'Skeeter' Rosemont still living out at the Richmond estate with his daughter. "I'm going to swing by the office and pick you up."

"I have a couple of other things you might be interested in too, Sheriff," Cari said. "I'll meet you out front."

Cari hopped in the Jeep a few minutes later and they drove toward the Richmond estate on the edge of town. It had only been a few years since Sharyn investigated the death of Julia's husband, Beau. The details of his murder had left the town in shock. Julia was twenty-three then, a beauty queen who married well and became the richest woman in the county.

"While I was checking out the Rosemont clan, I came across a few newspaper articles. Julia belonged to the Diamond Springs High School shooting club. She won a few awards. I couldn't find anything after high school. Maybe once a marksman, always a marksman? It was Barker Rosemont, Margaret's husband and Julia's uncle, Duke killed after the poker game when he won the Stag. It was ruled self-defense but Barker's brother, Skeeter, went after Duke later and was arrested for assault."

"Interesting family history," Sharyn remarked. "I wonder if Julia ever went after him."

"If she did, I couldn't find anything about it." Cari shuffled some papers. "That doesn't mean she didn't."

Sharyn followed the winding old road past the few farms left close in to the city. When she was a child, all of the land that surrounded Diamond Springs was farmland. Things had changed. Now most of it seemed to be shopping centers and subdivisions. Growth hadn't come in spurts for the area, it had come in a deluge.

She stopped the Jeep abruptly at the entrance to the long drive that led up to the old Richmond house. Agent Brewster was waiting next to his car. He flagged her down as she started to drive past him. How did he know she was headed that way? Not bothering to get out, she rolled down a window. "Agent Brewster."

"Sheriff Howard. You're dangerously close to messing up years of work in this area. You have no idea what you're doing. Back off now before any more damage is done."

"Agree to testify on behalf of my deputy and we've got a deal," she argued. "He's on his way to jail with no guarantee he'll make it to trial. Your investigation is interesting. I'd like to know who killed my father. But my deputy is alive and well right now. I want him to stay that way."

Brewster looked away for a moment, his eyes following the gentle slopes of the mountains in the distance. "You know I can't do that. Not unless we finish this investigation. And I can't guarantee when that will be. I can't save your deputy right now. But other people's lives could be in danger if you continue."

"I'm sorry, but I have a job to do. I hope it doesn't affect your case. If you'd like to give me more details on what to avoid, I'll be happy to try to work with you."

"I can't do that either. It's bad enough the investigation has been corrupted by Agent Gallagher. I can't afford another mistake."

"Then I'll do the best I can, Agent Brewster. I hope both of us get what we want."

"It's on *your* head now, Sheriff. Whatever happens, I hope you can live with it."

As Sharyn pulled the Jeep up the drive, Cari glanced back at the FBI agent. "Do you have any idea what he's talking about?"

"Maybe," Sharyn admitted. "We'll have to see."

Skeeter Rosemont met them at the door with Michaelson in tow. "You pay these fellas a fortune and they still can't get results."

"I'd like to ask you a few questions about your association with Duke Beatty," Sharyn told him. "I'd like to do it here but if not, we can go down to my office."

Skeeter wheezed as his wife and sister-in-law joined him. "I got nothin' to say to you, Sheriff. Everybody in these parts knows what happened to Barker. Duke killed him and stole our inheritance. Now he's dead. I don't feel bad takin' back what's rightfully mine."

Sharyn glanced at Amanda Rosemont. "What about Julia? What part did she play in this?"

Julia's mother grabbed her husband's arm. "She didn't have anything to do with this. It was personal between Duke and Skeeter."

"Shut your mouth, woman," her husband commanded. "You don't have to say anything."

"We know Julia was a good shooter in high school," Cari added. "Did you ask her to kill Duke or did she come up with that on her own?"

"Why not ask her yourself, Deputy." Julia's voice drifted with her perfume into the forty-foot foyer where they stood. "Are you accusing me of killing Duke Beatty?"

Sharyn faced her. "It might be helpful if you could tell us where you were when Duke was shot. I have this theory that David brought you to the speedway in his patrol car and waited for you while you took care of business. Since he never liked racing before, that's the only reason I can imagine him being at the track that morning. He follows you everywhere."

Julia's smile was a carefully created facial expression. "I was here all morning, Sheriff. You can ask anyone in this house. My family. The housekeeper. The cook. Any of them will swear I was here."

Sharyn thought back to what Marti said about people being willing to testify for Duke. "And I'd like to believe you, Mrs. Richmond. You've done a lot of good for the county. I know Nick will be devastated if we find out you killed Duke."

"Julia, keep quiet," her father advised. "Why bother having these fancypants lawyers if you're gonna stick your head out?"

"Shut up, Dad. Go upstairs. I'll call you if I need you. I don't need a lawyer. I haven't done anything wrong." Julia smiled at Sharyn again and handed her pocketbook to the butler. "Right, Sheriff? I mean, I wasn't on that tape, was I? Why aren't you accusing David of the crime?"

Sharyn glanced at the hat she held in her hands. David must have tipped her. She was prepared for them to be there. "I guess David forgot to tell you that he would've been *behind* the car when the shot was fired. The shot came from the office where you put Trudy to take the blame. You probably had David take Ed's rifle from his car. Even if Ed wasn't there you figured we'd blame it on Trudy since she had access to it."

"You're a masterful storyteller, Sheriff." Julia's sweet tone never wavered. "But this time, you've got it wrong. What could I possibly gain by killing Duke?"

"I was asking myself the same thing," Sharyn admitted, watching as Julia's family retreated only as far as the foot of the stairs. If Julia lost everything, so would they. The Rosemonts might have traded the world for the Stag-Inn-Doe. "I think it was personal. Getting Duke back for taking the Stag away from your family and killing your uncle. But there was another agenda too. I think someone besides you wanted Duke dead. Maybe Jack Winter?"

Julia walked toward her, removing her brown leather gloves as she spoke. "Sheriff, you've had some wild ideas in the past that you got lucky with. Trust me, this isn't one of them. Why don't you leave now before I have to call security?"

Cari put her hands on her hips and threw her shoulders back like a prize fighter. She kept the tips of her fingers on the handle of her pistol. "We're not leaving until we're ready, Mrs. Richmond. You don't seem to realize the seriousness of this charge."

Sharyn hid a small smile at her deputy's attitude. "It doesn't matter about the videotape. There was a trace of expensive European lipstick on the rifle stock. It was also on a cigarette butt we found at Duke's office. While we're speaking, the medical examiner's office is comparing that to your lipstick and saliva from a glass you left at the restaurant today. We should know in a few hours if they match."

Julia's gaze flew to her lawyer. "Is that legal?"

"Technically, if you leave something in a public place, it's not illegal," he admitted. "You shouldn't say anything else, Mrs. Richmond."

"This is stupid." Julia slapped her gloves on the palm of

her hand. "I'm going upstairs for a shower. We'll be talking about this at the next commission meeting, Sheriff."

"I think we'll be talking sooner than that," Sharyn told her. "Don't go anywhere. I'll let you know when I have word on that test."

Julia ignored her and sauntered upstairs past her family.

"We can't leave," Cari whispered. "What if she gets in her jet and takes off?"

"We aren't leaving." Sharyn put on her hat as she walked out the door. "We'll wait outside until we hear from Nick and Megan. She's not going anywhere."

They waited outside for almost two hours, enduring threatening looks from security officers and their dogs patrolling the estate. Sharyn's cell phone finally rang. It was Nick. "I hate you. You've probably stolen my only hope for a new van this year." He sighed. "The fingerprints on the Perrier bottle match Julia's prints on the water glass from the Palmer. We have a color match on the lipstick from the rifle, the cigarette butt and the water glass. It'll take longer for the complete chemical analysis but that's probably all you need to bring her in."

"Sorry," she apologized. "I like her too. But she killed Duke Beatty and tried to set up Trudy as the killer. Thanks for letting me know."

"Yeah. Well, you owe me about seventy thousand dollars from the sheriff's department budget to get a new van. I'll talk to you later. Be careful."

Sharyn closed her cell phone and looked at Cari. "Let's take her in."

"My favorite part," Cari quipped. "I love Miranda!"

"What do you mean she's gone?" Sharyn demanded when she was called to the DA's office the next morning. She'd brought a whining, irritated Julia Richmond in to spend the night in the county lockup. The lipstick analysis came through during the night. She matched up on all counts. A quick search of her house found the pale pink silk blouse whose fibers matched the ones on the circle of glass she'd cut from the window to shoot Duke.

"Calm yourself, Sheriff." Mr. Percy sat back in his chair and waited for her to sit down. "Your deputy has been exonerated. Before the FBI claimed her as a material witness in an investigation, she signed this confession." He showed her the document that named Julia as Duke's killer and an accomplice in Gunther's death and Trudy's kidnapping.

Sharyn examined the paper. "Where is she now?"

He shrugged gracefully. "I'm not privileged to that information. Suffice it to say, you got what you wanted. Mrs. Robinson and your deputy are free. We can't prosecute David for his crime. Mrs. Richmond is more valuable to the federal government than to us."

"This wraps everything up nice and neat," she accused, "without providing any embarrassing explanations."

Mr. Percy's sharp blue eyes focused on her. "What do you mean?"

"I mean, you and Jack Winter trying to keep Caison from helping Ed. I mean the *real* reason Duke was killed, not the popular idea that the Rosemonts wanted the Stag-Inn-Doe."

"Be careful, Sheriff," Percy warned. "You may be treading on unusually thin ice in this matter. I'd hate to see you hurt. Or worse."

Sharyn put her hands on his desk and faced him. "Be honest with me, Mr. Percy. Tell me what Julia Richmond's part was in all of this."

Before he could answer, his phone rang. He picked up the receiver then handed it to her. "It's for you. I'm late for court."

"Sharyn, it's David." Ernie's voice was frantic. "We're out at that new subdivision off Main Street, near the edge of town. Hurry!"

She put down the phone and stared for an instant into Percy's cold eyes. "I'm not going away, sir. I can't be bought. I'll find the answers."

* * *

The paramedics were already putting David into the back of the ambulance by the time Sharyn got there. Ernie and Joe were there with him. Ed was still on the way back from the county jail.

"What happened?" Sharyn asked her deputies when she saw the blood on the orange clay. The steady rain was already washing away any evidence of the crime.

"The chief said he got a call. Someone was trying to break into a house out here. David came out and somebody shot him." Ernie nodded at the ambulance. "Chief's on his way out. It doesn't look good."

"Shouldn't he have been on desk duty pending the investigation?" she demanded, already knowing how it happened. "Could David identify the shooter?"

"I don't know," Ernie answered. "He said he didn't see anybody. He was walking through the yard. He wasn't wearing a vest."

The paramedic interrupted them. "Sheriff, he's asking for you."

Sharyn went to kneel beside the stretcher in the ambulance. David was soaked and bloody, his dark hair plastered to his forehead, tubes running from his arms. She took his hand in hers. He was freezing. "You should go. They need to get you to the hospital."

He laughed. "I saw the way Ernie looked at me. I know I'm going to die. I just wanted you to know I did it so you'd be proud of me."

"What are you saying, David? What did you do?"

"I wanted everyone to be proud of me. That's why I helped the FBI with Julia. I was so close to finding the real players, you know?"

The paramedic nudged Sharyn. "We have to go."

"You'll be all right," she told David. "You'll see. Just hold on. You can make it. Everyone's proud of you."

He smiled but didn't respond. Sharyn squeezed his hand then climbed out of the ambulance. It pulled away leaving the rest of them standing in the rain and the fog.

Epilogue

They buried David Matthews three days later with full honors. The funeral procession was long, winding up the side of Diamond Mountain where the small church his family attended held the burial services.

Sharyn stood beside the casket as it was lowered into the ground. David's mother was sobbing in Ed's arms with a tearful Trudy standing beside him. She noticed Agent Brewster on the sidelines of the large group. Not waiting for him to disappear into the crowd, she confronted him. "You got him tangled up in this, didn't you?"

Brewster raised his chin to look at her. "I warned you. These people don't play games. David wasn't useful to them anymore. What did you think was going to happen?"

"But you still don't know who killed him or why he was killed."

"We'll find out, Sheriff. It might take us some time—"

"I'm through waiting for you. This whole operation of yours has been run slipshod." She controlled her voice so it didn't crack. "You say you've been after Jack Winter and the others all these years and all you can show for it is this funeral and my stolen book. A good man is dead. I'll find out who killed him. That's the only way I see David getting any justice."

She walked away from him, not waiting for an answer,

182

and was enmeshed in the mourning group of David's family, friends and co-workers.

Joe approached her in his dress uniform, for once minus his sunglasses. "I'm sorry to have to break this to you right now, Sharyn, but I've been called up for active duty in the Middle East. I knew it could happen. I'm not as young as some of them but I've got this expertise from the last time. My unit needs me again."

She put her suddenly shaking hands into her pockets. *Not Joe. Not now.* "When do you leave?"

"Twenty-four hours. Sorry there wasn't more notice. I hope you all will check in on Sarah for me while I'm gone."

"You know we will. Don't worry about a thing going on here." She hugged him, trying to be as strong as he was. "Be careful. Make sure you come back to us."

"I will. You take care."

Sharyn watched him walk away through the mountain mist as the first shovel of dirt was thrown on David's coffin. She was afraid there was going to be a long, cold winter ahead.